A LITTLE DISCOVERY

MANOR DRIVE
BOOK ONE

KATE BAUER

CONTENT WARNING

This book contains graphic depictions/descriptions/recollections of Sexual Assault, homophobic slurs, suicidal ideations, family abandonment, racism, and mention of conversion camps and a failed restraining order.

Discretion is advised.

INTRODUCTION

Manor Drive is a secluded street, set atop a cliff and surrounded by forest, a mere twenty minutes outside of the city. The only way to reach it is the steep drive behind the roadside bar, McKinley's Tavern. The steep angle of the road, and its ascent into the woods, seem to be enough to deter the average person from trespassing. It is at the end of the road that you will find a large manor house, shared by like minded young people... the house lovingly referred to as "Kink Manor."

The neighborhood on the hill used to be a trailer park back in the day, until the local landfill bought them out and forced the residents to leave. However, the company went bankrupt and the landfill covered before the grounds of the property were ever disturbed. For years, it sat empty and abandoned, nature trying to reclaim where homes once stood... until an anonymous buyer snatched it up at auction.

Within months, the road to the left of the hilltop was

revamped into a modern mobile home court, housing a dozen brand new homes. The road to the right, however, became the private drive for the manor house. The house is a newer addition, added only five years ago, shortly after the bar at the bottom of the hill changed ownership.

No one really knows who owns the small neighborhood on top of the hill, nor the bar next to the highway, but one thing is for certain... as long as it's legal, you're expected to let your freak flag fly.

1

LUCKY

"Lucas, I'm pregnant."

The coffee I spent my last five dollars in my wallet on goes spewing out of my mouth, all over the girl who just popped up in front of me. She looks vaguely familiar, like I might have class with her or something, but for the life of me, I cannot recall a name. Her voice makes me want to call her Cruella. She seems like someone who would want to skin puppies for a coat.

While she wipes at her face, I hurriedly set down my overpriced, wonderfully over sugared cup of magic bean juice to dig out my handkerchief from my backpack. Grandfather always said that I needed to carry one, that tissues were too plebian for anything other than snot. A handkerchief is the only acceptable thing to have on hand when you needed to assist a damsel in distress... My father's side of the family doesn't believe in the poor.

"They just don't try hard enough..."

The girl snatches the piece of cloth from my hands without hesitation, her nails drawing blood on the back of my hand. I *almost* manage to hold back the whimper, but I have never done well with the sight of blood. I am getting better at not fainting at the sight of my own blood, but it still makes me want to curl up and cry. If someone else is bleeding? Find me a flat surface pronto because it will be lights out in under a minute.

I kind of wish I didn't give her my hanky so I could wrap my hand, but I was raised to be a gentleman. The offensive snot pockets, more commonly known as tissues to those who don't think like my relatives, will have to suffice for cleaning up my blood. I guess it's better this way since bloodstains are harder to remove than coffee most of the time...

"You were the only one I have been with, Lucas, so it has to be yours. You have to make this right!"

Oh, she is still talking?

It's a struggle not to laugh in her face. How in the world could I put a baby in her?

Number one: I have never had sex... Not with a woman. Not with a man. Not even with a dolly. Gramps on my mother's side has like four or five illegitimate kids, and I want none of that drama.

Number two: The thought of even touching a vagina is enough to make me laugh uncontrollably. No offense to the ladies of the world, but every time I read a romance novel that talks about a beautiful blooming flower, I giggle. Some of those books make visits to the botanical gardens a hoot. My parents stopped dragging me to the charity events there after I couldn't stop laughing at the rose bushes.

And number three: I'm pretty certain I am asexual. The act itself is just not that appealing to me.

"LUCAS ANTHONY HOLLOWAY!"

Shit! Why is my mother on campus?!

"Did I just hear that you got a girl pregnant, and you are ignoring your responsibilities?" my mother scolds me like I'm a toddler and not the nineteen-year-old man that I am. Sometimes I hate being born into this family. I can't cough at a fundraiser, but she can throw a tantrum in the middle of the campus on the sidewalk. Sounds about right.

An hour later, I am not in class like I should be. Instead, I'm on the sofa in my father's den while my mother is still going on and on about her half-siblings and how they ruined her life. For the most part, my father is merely staring at the crazy woman, nodding in the appropriate places, but in reality, he's likely doing calculations in his head to figure out the cost breakdown of his options if this were to get out to the media. He's nothing, if not a shrewd businessman.

I have already done my own calculations. I have two options here. Either I fight the accusations of this girl, and create a gossip storm about the heir of Holloway Industries abandoning his baby mama... Or, I marry her, and raise the kid as my own, saving them from the puppy

3

wearing monstrosity that is carrying him or her. There really is no choice for me if I want to avoid the conflict raging around me...

"Call the lawyers," I pipe up, interrupting my mother's rant about one of my uncles ruining her sixteenth birthday by having the audacity to be born and pull her father away from her special day.

"We'll do a pre-nup and then I'll marry her so the baby is legitimate. I won't let the child be born a bastard."

That last part is solely for my mother's benefit, so that she would shut the hell up about bastards and inheritances. In truth, my mother couldn't care less about her half-siblings if it wasn't for the money. Gramps is worth billions... with a capital B... and my mother seems to think because she is his only legitimate child she deserves all of it. Nevermind the fact that she married my father, whose company is worth millions. She wants every penny. I think if she ever found a way to cut me off, she would do it.

The look my father gives me is one of pity. He knows that this girl is cut from the same cloth as my mother. He knows she is only after me for my money. Sad part is, it isn't even my money. I'm their only kid, so I guess all of this crap eventually becomes mine someday, whether I want it or not. I would trade all the money in the world for some peace and quiet right about now. Mother has called the girl and arranged for the lawyer and an officiant to meet at the house tomorrow. Looks like we aren't wasting any time.

June

It has been a month or so since I lost my favorite hanky to this girl, not to mention my freedom. Her name is apparently Sabrina Carlisle, and we supposedly slept together at a party months ago. I vaguely recall the party, but sure as hell don't remember losing my virginity.

It was the one and only time my roommate managed to drag me out of our dorm room, but I didn't stay very long... or rather I wasn't conscious very long. Shortly after we arrived at the frat house, someone took a header down the stairs. When I saw the blood, one of the brothers in the house led me to his room to lie down. I was about thirty seconds from lights out when he found me.

According to Sabrina and James, my roommate, she went in the room to lie down after drinking too much without realizing I was in there. Supposedly, we hit it off and one thing led to another. I know it was all lies, but it was an easy sell to my mother, who trapped my father by being pregnant with me. My father, on the other hand, didn't believe a word of it; hence, the pre-nup.

The terms of the pre-nuptial agreement are cut and dry. If I die, she gets nothing. My father insisted on that one. Apparently, one of his college buddies almost got taken out when his new wife tried to hire a hit man, only she hired an undercover cop instead. Father told me many times as a teenager to be wary of gold diggers. I'm pretty sure he has mother followed and under surveillance now.

If Sabrina and I divorce amicably or through no fault, we each leave with whatever we brought into the marriage and all assets are distributed according to whose funds were used to purchase them. In other words, if my inheritance or income pays for things, they are mine and not joint property. That one had to go through the lawyers because in some states, there are special rules for distribution of property and such after a divorce.

Pretty much the only way she gets anything is if she can *prove* infidelity on my part. Considering I am on hundred percent certain that I am still a virgin with no intention of changing that fact, she's trapped in this marriage just as much as I am if she wants the money.

It didn't escape my notice that she, a longtime friend of my roommate, suddenly shows up "pregnant" after James figured out that I was part of *that* Holloway family. He saw a news article online with a photo from the last family gathering. It was the company's seventy-five-year anniversary, so I had to be there with my parents. I hate events like that. But for my father's sake, I attend them with the fakest smile possible and make a game out of avoiding the cameras. I guess luck wasn't on my side that night and I just so happened to be in the background getting some food in the picture posted with the article.

Thanks to that one photo, I am stuck in a marriage with a shrew of a woman and someone else's kid on the way. I always wanted to be a dad, but figured it would be difficult to get a kid when I can't get it up with another person. So getting the kid without the sex is a huge plus for me. That is honestly the only highlight of this entire fiasco. There's something to be said about wanting to give someone else what you never got to have yourself. This kid will get all the affection in the world from me. He or she won't ever have to question whether or not their dad loves them.

"Of course, you will have to give up school and start working," my mother's voice snaps me back to the conversation at hand. "You cannot stay in the dorms now that you are a married man, and although your father and I will gift you a house, you will need to earn the money to support your family yourself. You *are* an adult now, Lucas. You'll just have to withdraw from going back in the fall."

I know my mouth is gaping open due to the surprise. What is she going on about? What kind of job could I possibly manage to get with a high school diploma that would support me and the gold-digger in a house that she picks out as adequate? Anything less than twelve rooms is unacceptable in her eyes...

"Mother," my new wife croons. "A house would be absolutely lovely! I'm sure Lucas wants to start right away. My father even offered him an executive position at our family's business, but he was worried about it interfering with school. We didn't want to abandon something you all worked so hard for."

Am I living in an alternate universe? They want me to not only quit school, but to work for my father-in-law, whom I've never met, doing God only knows what. I look to my father in horror, but he has just buried his head in whatever is on his tablet. I know he cares in his own way, but it has always been more important to keep the peace than to do what is right when it comes to him. He doesn't even try to offer me a position at Holloway Industries to counter what the women are deciding for my life.

"That sounds wonderful, dear," Mother says sweetly to Sabrina. "Carlisle Construction is such a good up and coming company. I just know that with my son as an executive, it will become the elite contracting choice in the city in no time."

There it is. My future is resting on making a construction company owned by my new in-laws into a success... A company that last I saw was on the brink of bankruptcy and had so many consumer complaints against it that the only way they managed to stay afloat was random influxes of cash over the years.

At least I'll have the kid to give me a bright spot in my life because my future just got bleak as fuck.

2

LUCKY

She lost the baby... Sure, she did. My mother and Sabrina are bawling their eyes out over a kid that I am quite positive at this point never even existed.

I'm not stupid. A lot of the people in my life think I am, but they mistake non-confrontational and quiet as a lack of intelligence. I am fully aware of all of the times people are trying to manipulate me or use me to get money. There is no hiding the fact that every single one of my so-called friends disappeared the second I stopped paying for things. My new wife is just as bad as Mother when it comes to sharing wealth.

Initially, I was surprised that the alleged miscarriage didn't happen right after we were married. Then I took a closer look at the pre-nup which says that we had to be married and cohabitating for at least ninety days to fulfill the requirements of the annulment clause. She really did a good job of reading the fine print. She also had to sign documents agreeing to a paternity test in order to fulfill another one of the clauses my father put in. If the baby turned out to be someone else's, the marriage would be terminated and she would face fraud charges.

After the last three months of working for my father-in-law, nothing Sabrina does surprises me. There is a very valid reason Carlisle Construction hasn't been overly successful... My in-laws are con artists. They consistently swap out materials for cheaper options, while charging for the more expensive ones. Their laborers are all third-party contractors, some of whom aren't even licensed or trained properly to do the work they are asked to do. It's a total shit show.

And I am responsible for customer satisfaction... I would turn them in if I could afford to pay the breach of the NDA I had to sign. I can't even get a call through to my father's attorney to check on its legality because Mother told them to cut me off completely.

I spend every waking moment fielding calls and emails, complaining about the company and the shoddy work. It has become my responsibility to offer rebates and refunds to compensate out of my own pocket, because although my parents have cut me off, they released my trust fund early. My trust fund was released by my mother, but with a stipulation that I had to invest in Carlisle Construction. The money that was supposed to keep me comfortable until retirement, over twenty million dollars, is almost all spent to support the lying bitch and her criminal family.

I managed to squirrel away about two hundred thousand dollars before Sabrina and my in-laws got their hands on my trust account. It's not much, but it should be more than enough that I can start over when she inevitably drops my ass.

Please, God, let it be soon...

***

May

Pulling into the parking lot of the motel, I'm glad that James is at the house with Sabrina. The two of them are fucking like bunnies, but I still don't give a shit. I have tried to set things up to where I can catch her in the act of infidelity just so I can get a quickie divorce, but either she somehow pays off the investigator, or they can't get legal access to the house security systems for observation. There's something about how they need all of the owners' permission or something.

So, when they stopped hiding what they were doing from me, I started to come here. It's a bit seedy looking on the outside, but the rooms are clean and the guy at the desk is nice. Plus, they offer cartoon and anime streaming services in the rooms included with your room fee. Sabrina thinks that childish things like that aren't appropriate for a grown man, so she cancelled all of my subscriptions, not that I could afford them anymore with what she leaves me from my paychecks.

Between the money, activities ban, and the diet, I need this break. I hadn't had pizza or chocolate in over six months before I found this place. I can afford one night every other week without Sabrina noticing, so I take full advantage of her trysts with James. A few hours twice a month to not feel like a doormat or ATM card... that's all I need. My rainy day account still has enough to start over.

Eventually she will get sick of me and the lack of fresh money. Eventually, I'll be free of her. But for now, I pick up my usual room key from the guy at the desk and hand him his small pizza. I need some cartoon therapy pretty desperately.

3

SPENCER

My side hustle email address is showing another new message. I already know who it is from. Sabrina Carlisle has been on my case for months to follow her husband around so that she can divorce him. She *says* he is cheating and she needs proof. Honestly, if the guy is cheating, good on him. I would, too, if I was married to her. Usually, I can't wait to catch the adulterous asswipes, but I've known Sabrina since kindergarten... I pity the man who married her.

I mark the email as read without even opening it just so that the alert goes away. I have zero intention of taking the job. I may be one of the newer private investigators in the county, but that doesn't mean I will abandon my morals, or subject myself to verbal harassment from a client...

My school email alerts that I've got a new message from Professor Michaels. This could be something infinitely better, and my mood starts to improve drastically. I hurry to open the message and begin to read:

From: apmichaels@wrenshaw.edu

To: swright@wrenshaw.edu

Subject: Photography Abroad Program

Dear Mr. Wright,

Congratulations!

You have been accepted to the cross-continental photography program. The continent you have been selected to visit for a month is Australia. Your lodgings and travel are included in the fees to be paid upon acceptance. You are responsible for your own food, supplies, and any fees or taxes associated with customs.

Please be advised that the active dates of the course start on July 18 and will conclude on August 18. Your travel arrangements will be scheduled within five days before and after the active course dates.

You must respond by Wednesday, so that we can book your air travel and lodgings for the duration of the course.

Please complete the attached form to register your acceptance and contact the registrar with the confirmation number of 583928 to submit payment.

Good luck!

Dr. Aaron Michaels

Professor of the Arts - Photography and Photojournalism

HOLY SHIT!

I got in!

I let out a yell of triumph, only to have four different guys come racing into the lounge where I am sitting on the couch. I set my laptop on the end table and open my arms for the dog pile. Subsequently, I get buried under the four men in a celebratory puppy pile. They all knew I was waiting on this kind of a break. Photography is my passion, so this is fucking huge for me.

Eric is the first to stand back up, adjusting the bralette camisole he's wearing in place of a shirt today. Bending over at the waist, he moves his ass into position to tease me while he reads the email. I know he's practicing for his drag show act later tonight, but he really does have an amazing set of assets back there. If only he was less of a brat, there could be something. But we've talked it out a few times over the years of our friendship. He needs a heavy-handed Dom, where I'm more of a cuddle and comfort Daddy Dom.

As the other guys adjust themselves onto the cuddle puddle we typically form in the parlor area, Eric flops into the recliner and says, "Have you called to find out if your scholarship will cover the cost?"

The smile falls from my face and I whip my head around to look at him. I know the trip is like seven thousand dollars, and I had assumed that what I had leftover in my scholarship would cover it considering it is a school sponsored trip, but what if it isn't? And food for a month... That's at least a grand right there.

Glancing at the clock, I have about fifteen minutes until the registrar closes for the weekend. Throwing Toby off of my lap, I give him a small smile of apology before grabbing my phone. Hitting the seventeen million different numbers to get through the automated system to the registrar's office, I pray they didn't decide to start their weekend early...

"Registrar's office," a soft voice answers when I'm about to give up. "How can I help you?"

"I am doing the photography abroad program and need to know if my scholarship will cover the cost," I say in a hurry. I don't want to waste their time, but I need to know. I only have until Wednesday to claim my spot in the program.

"Student number?" they ask. "Each scholarship has stipulations attached, so I can't make a blanket state-ment. I *do* know that the program will accept scholarship funds, but without looking at your file, I cannot say if *yours* will allow funds to pay for a program such as this."

I give her my student ID number and wait while I hear the clacking of keys on a keyboard. Looking at the clock on our wall, I watch the seconds tick away. In my experience, the closer it gets to quitting time, the less expedient and efficient a person gets at work. At least, that's what my father used to say.

"Mr. Wright?" the voice on the phone brings me back to the call before more of my memories can take over. "It appears the stipulations of your scholarship will only cover fifty percent of the cost of the program due to the fact that the program has you traveling internationally. Do you want me to apply the funds and take the rest of the payment today?"

My heart drops as I realize I will have to figure out a way to come up with at least five grand for this program, most of it in under a week, or give up my spot.

"I don't have the additional payment just yet," I tell them to buy some time. "Can I have the weekend to rearrange some funds?"

"Of course, Mr. Wright," the voice says. I can hear the sympathy in their tone, and it grates my nerves. "I will put you down to be contacted on Tuesday morning if we don't hear from you before then. That way if you are unable to attend the program, Professor Michaels has the time to fill your spot with an alternate."

I mumble some sort of appreciation before disconnecting the call. How in the fuck am I supposed to come up with five grand in under five days?

The email alert for my private investigations business lights up again.

Can I deal with the bitch for the sake of not missing this chance of a lifetime? Yes. Yes, I can.

4

SPENCER

__August__

Packing up my equipment is a bittersweet feeling. I spent the last four weeks traipsing across the Australian outback, capturing wildlife and landscape shots I would have only dreamed of before. The professor over here taught us all how to use weather forecasts and the natural timing of the day to create visuals I previously believed were only available through photoshop. It's been a completely surreal experience.

"You ready to get back to your tiny ass city?" my roommate for the trip, Stan, asks me while zipping up his own suitcase. "You are always welcome to join me and my brothers in Atlanta if you get sick of the cold."

He shivers a bit while glancing outside. I laugh as my head turns the same direction. It's crazy to think that I'm seeing snow in August, but that is what happens when you're in a different hemisphere. As much as I have fallen in love with this place, I can't imagine not wearing ugly sweaters on Christmas.

Even with my folks gone, I continue the tradition. The guys back home help me remember them...

I shake my head to dislodge the morose thoughts before I start gathering up the last of my stuff. We travel by road to Sydney in the morning and will catch our flights back to our home areas. Stan and I will part ways at LAX. He will fly off to The Big A while I head to Pittsburgh.

I'm not looking forward to the cost for a rideshare home from the airport, but I want to surprise the guys. It's been a long month away from my found family at Kink Manor, and I know they feel my absence as much as I feel theirs... I know it because of the emails I've been receiving from our beloved self-appointed HBIC, head brat in charge. Eric has kept me updated on everything, whether I want to know it or not.

One thing I wish I could have an update on is the job I did for Sabrina Carlisle. She seemed way too happy about the pictures I delivered to her. All they showed that her husband doing was nothing more than pigging out on pizza and junk food while watching cartoons. I don't think the guy is even capable of an affair, unless the person was covered in mozzarella and pepperoni, because the only thing he was interested in was the food and the television.

I provided a comprehensive report and filed the case with the agency I had my investigations license through.

That way, if called, I could testify in court. Considering the process for divorce from filing to the hearing usually takes at least three months or longer, there shouldn't be any way for her to screw the guy over at this point. Her joy just left a bad taste in my mouth that I haven't been able to get rid of.

"Lights out!" the program director's voice calls out, and I reach for the switch. Soon, I will be in my own bed again...

5

LUCKY

On the bright side, at least I'm divorced now. Leaving the shrew in the rear view is yet another reason that I am driving away from the city proper right now.

It took a little under a year for Sabrina to completely blow through my inheritance. After that, once it was clear my family wasn't giving me any more money, she found a way to frame me for adultery. I didn't make that too difficult for her since I was regularly showing up at the same motel over and over again. But any investigator with a third-grade education would see that I was there alone every time.

As much as I love the whole pizza man porno trope, acne prone teenagers are not my type. The pizza delivery was no-contact every single time, if I even ordered delivery at all. Most of the time, I did carryout and brought it with me.

Even with testimony from Chris, the guy at the desk for the motel, saying that I was alone, she still managed to convince a judge that I was unfaithful because of the photographs provided by the investigator. The guy was subpoenaed but was a no-show to the hearing. The judge ruled in my ex-wife's favor, and she took it all. That was a week ago.

Obviously, my father-in-law fired me. Thank the heavens... And thanks to Sabrina telling anyone and everyone in my family that I cheated and that's how she won the divorce, the whole city thinks I'm a lying, cheating, asshole. Then there's my mother. Apparently, I am just like her father and have no sense of familial loyalty.

My father won't hire me with my mother in full on hate mode against me. Just once, I would like to see the man whose house I grew up in stand up to the woman who gave birth to me. But, no. He would rather publicly disown me and make it impossible for me to get *any* job worth having in the city.

Now, I'm down to the last two hundred dollars that I have available from my liquidated stash. I only had about ten thousand of the two hundred liquidated so far. When I got the divorce papers, I figured I would have more time. I thought that the discovery process would take longer and that my bank account was still secret. I was wrong on both parts. The pre-nuptial agreement made things very cut and dry. As for the account, Sabrina apparently knew about it from the beginning.

Two hundred dollars is a far cry from the twenty million I had. Technically, whatever is left in the accounts should be getting split fifty-fifty, but my ex-wife's lawyer argued that since I was the one who was unfaithful, the pre-nup was unjustly weighted in my favor and that the same rules applied to her should apply to me. The judge hasn't made a ruling on that part just yet, so he's frozen the accounts until he does. Unfortunately for me, that just means I'm stuck without a place to sleep, or anything but the few clothes and personal belongings I managed to fit into the car I acquired.

I was hoping that I could get a cheap car to replace the one Sabrina took in the divorce and then use the rest of the ten grand to pay for the next semester of school, but that was a pipe dream. The car ended up costing me almost seven grand when the taxes and title fees got added in. The three grand that was left wouldn't pay for tuition and room and board for school. Hell, it doesn't even pay for full time tuition for a semester. I can only afford two courses and have nowhere to live.

There was a chance I could stay with Gramps outside of the city, but Mother apparently made her feelings clear to the entire family. I've already heard it from the aunts, uncles, and cousins on Father's side. Last I heard, Mother had just came back from visiting with Gramps, so I'm sure he knows now. I don't think I could handle him being disappointed in me, even though I did nothing wrong other than marrying a girl just to shut her up. I already feel enough shame over it. I don't need to add being a disappointment to the only person who I ever wanted to make proud.

At least it's the end of summer. With the tent I managed to find on clearance, I should be able to find some woods somewhere that no one will report me... at least until I can find a job that will pay enough for a room to rent.

As I drive past what used to be the grocery store Gramps took me to when I was little, my car starts shaking and making a horrible knocking noise. *This can't be happening...*

I can somewhat make out a sign glowing in the darkness up ahead and start the prayers that I can make it. Maybe this McKinley's Tavern will be good luck for me?

The snort of laughter turns into a choked sob as my engine dies two hundred feet or so away from the parking lot. I drift my car to the shoulder of the highway and lay my head down onto the wheel. Letting the pain of the last sixteen months take over, I scream and sob in my broken down junker car, cursing the universe and everyone and everything in my life.

Lucas Anthony Holloway, heir to the Holloway fortune, is a nothing but a loser. Maybe if no one knows who I am, I might have a chance to be happy for once in my life.

"Lucky, my boy, you have a bright future ahead of you."

Sure thing, Gramps. He may have given me the nickname of Lucky, but it hasn't helped me at all in this life. Lucas Holloway is the unluckiest boy who ever lived. Lucky Hollow might have better luck.

I sit back upright and pull a hanky out of the pocket of my backpack to wipe my face as best I can. I never did get my favorite one back from Sabrina, but that's alright. Lucky doesn't need reminders of Lucas's life.

Locking the door to my apparent oversized lawn decoration, I start the trek to the bar and pray that they're open. If nothing else, I can wait in relative safety for the tow truck that will take my last two hundred dollars from me.

6

LUCKY

The bar is more crowded than I expected based on the number of cars I could see out front. Of course, the door slamming behind me causes every eye to turn my way. As if I didn't feel like enough of a loser, the bartender throws his rag down and stomps over to me.

This is just what I should expect. I am going to get kicked out of here and have to sleep in my car on the side of the highway where I will probably get crushed by a tractor trailer when the driver falls asleep at the wheel and...

"Who hurt you?" the voice in front of me growls out.

I look up, and I mean *UP* into the face of the bartender and can't stop my chin from wobbling. I'm just so tired of pretending I have my shit together. I just want to let go for once...

"Jace!" another voice rings out from across the room. "You're scaring the kid, ya big oaf!"

The bartender, Jace, looks behind him and then back

at me. He must see something on my face because he immediately crouches in front of me and does some sort of magic, transforming himself from fierce biker enforcer who will make you disappear for insulting his mama's spaghetti sauce and becoming a cuddly teddy bear who can make all the boo-boos go away. I can't handle the change and start to back away.

The car is looking like a better alternative to whatever this is. I know I'm on the verge of a panic attack. I get them multiple times a day now. I need to get away. They can't see the real me. No one sees the real me... not anymore...

The bar is suspiciously silent as I try to keep everyone in my sights. They're all staring at me. I feel like a freak show, just like Sabrina always says I am. They judge me without knowing me. They don't want to know me. They just want to see the little trust fund boy make a fool of himself.

"Fuck!" a lady, no wait that's a guy in drag, calls out. "Eli, you got a towel? My compact broke in my purse and I got my finger."

I watch in horror as he starts to pull his hand out of the bag. If he needs a towel, that means there's blood. I can't stay and see it! I want to run, but my feet won't move. I'm glued to the spot, frozen and locked on to the image of his arm slowly pulling free of the purse.

At the first sight of the garish red liquid, I feel the floaty sensation that precedes my body making fast friends with the floor. Glancing down, the only thought in my head is, *at least it looks like they mop in here* before my vision blacks out completely and I'm lost to the darkness.

I am not sure how much time passes before I regain consciousness, but the first sign that it wasn't a dream is the fact that I hear arguing about whether or not to take me to a hospital.

"No hospital," I manage to mumble before I can muster the energy to open my eyes. I'm still trying to catalogue what was real and what was my imagination before I passed out.

Based on the smell of stale beer and lemon cleaner, I can safely assume the bar is real. That means that the werewolf biker bartender and the drag queen are likely real as well... Well fuck a duck that's just swell.

Laughter and giggles surround me before the voice I recognize as the drag queen speaks up, "He thinks you're a werewolf, Jace."

Another round of laughter and light slaps follow. The sounds make me want to see all of these people who are obviously good friends. I've never had that before... I don't think I have even seen it outside of television before.

"There you are," says a voice from above my head as I open my eyes. Tilting my head up, I see the man who had come out of the back room to scold the werewolf...er... bartender.

He puts his arms under my armpits to help me up

into a sitting position while everyone else takes a few steps back. Looking around the room, it appears that the bar has emptied out except for these people. And they certainly look like an interesting bunch.

There's the guy helping me. He looks like he's a de-facto leader. There is something about him that makes me feel safe in a way that only Gramps ever did. I can't put my finger on what it is, but judging by his soft smile, he is glad that I'm up and awake.

The giant bartender, Jace, is hanging back, trying to hide behind a guy half his size. He really does make me want to snuggle him, but not in a weird way. Now that he's not all growly, he seems shy. Even with the tattoos and beard and scars, he looks like me passing out really scared him. The smaller guy in front of him turns around to wrap him up in a bear hug which brings a smile to the bigger man's face.

The smaller guy looks like he belongs in front of a computer screen, big ole black plastic framed glasses and all. I don't know what the relationship is between the two of them, but I'm not getting sexy vibes from them.

Same goes for the two guys to my right. They seem to be holding each other, but there's only comfort vibes radiating off of them. I have to do a double take to make sure I'm not dreaming, but they are both wearing collars, like legit pet collars with tags. And is that a headband with dog ears?

I lay back down to close my eyes and count to ten. This *has* to be a dream.

"Ain't no dream, sweetheart."

I open my eyes and let out a squeak. The drag queen is in full regalia leaning over me. Apparently, I was out long enough for him to finish his makeup and wardrobe change.

"Kid, if you ain't comfortable with what you're seeing here, you came to the wrong place," he says as he saunters off to perch on one of the bar stools. "Mac's and Manor Drive ain't for no small minded bigots."

"Eric, put Miss Sassy Frass away until I can at least make sure he doesn't have a concussion, please," the safety guy says to the drag queen. Turning to me, he asks, "Did you hit your head at all before coming in here? Do you know what caused you to pass out?"

I look back and forth between the man and the queen and the only thing I can manage to get out is, "Sassy Frass? More like Brat-ney Bitch."

I slap my hand over my mouth and pray that I'm not about to get my ass beat. My brain to mouth filter usually doesn't disappear unless heavy alcohol consumption involved... Why the fuck did I just say that?!

"Oh, you're going to fit in just fine, darlin," Eric aka Sassy tells me with a wink. "I might just use that one of these days."

Cackling, the queen gets up from her stool and makes her way out a door in the back of the room. From the quick glance I catch before it closes, I notice that must be where the other cars were. Parking in the rear...

I let out a giggle due to the stress and lower my hand from my mouth. Safety guy gives me a smile and responding chuckle before helping me up again. Before I can forget my manners, I hold out my hand to him to introduce myself, "Lucky Hollow is the name, and I broke down up the road a bit. No bumps or bruises unless I hit something on the way down or smacked my head off the floor. I'm just not so good when I see blood."

"I *thought* you looked familiar!" the one with the puppy ears yells out, making me scooch back practically into safety guy's lap. "You were the one who used Spencer's old room at the Theta party back before he moved in with us!"

"Inside voice, Toby," the guy behind me chides gently.

"Sorry, Eli," Toby replies, not sounding sorry at all because he's way too excited. "Everyone was teasing him about you so much! He kept wanting to go check on you every five minutes, but his fraternity brothers kept him in Daddy mode for them all night. You were gone by the time he got back up there."

The reminder of the night that ruined my life is just too much. Even with how wonderful these guys are being to me, I can't stop the feelings inside of me. A choking noise comes from my throat as I bury my head in my hands to sob uncontrollably.

7

LUCKY

Eli sets me on a chair in the back office while he goes back out to the bar to kick everyone out and close up. It's still early by bar standards, but he explained that the owner would rather lose the sales from a couple of drunk randos at one in the morning than have his employees sitting in an empty building on the side of the highway for an extra three hours. When he carries the cash drawer into the office, I get up to leave.

"Do you need the restroom?" he asks as he opens the safe, not caring at all that I could have been watching. I mean, I wasn't, but still...

I shake my head which he somehow manages to see even with his back to me. His response is a chuckle and a pointed finger to the chair I just vacated. For some reason, I obey him and sit. Maybe it's just the fact that I'm exhausted...Then again, it is likely the fact that obedience for the sake of expediency and avoiding conflict has been how I have survived this life.

It's also how I got myself into this fucked up situation...

My inner thoughts suck donkey patootie...

Eli's chuckle as he closes the safe makes me realize that last thought wasn't kept in my head.

"No, Lucky," he says, reaching for my hand and pulling me to my feet. "Your thoughts aren't staying in your head very well tonight it seems."

I follow the man as he pulls me out of the office and down the hall to an alarm panel. There, he punches in a code, again not caring that I am there. Is he wanting the place to get robbed?

"If I was worried about you robbing the place, I would be in a padded room somewhere for paranoia, little one," he says as he pulls me through the back door before turning to lock the deadbolt with a key. "You look like you would confess to things you didn't even do, just to stop the questions. Am I right?"

Embarrassed at the accuracy of his observations, I nod and hang my head. Eli puts his index finger under my chin and raises it so that I meet his gaze. He's taller than I am, but only by an inch or so. Yet the aura he exudes makes me feel like I'm looking up to the top of a mountain.

"There is nothing wrong with wanting to avoid conflict, Lucky," he tells me. "But if the choice is between conflict and a lie, then you *need* to fight."

He moves his finger from under my chin and heads for the only car left in the lot. Since my time of safety has run out, I bite the bullet and figure I can at least ask him for his advice. He seems to know a lot about people.

"What do you do when it's too late to fight and the lie has become truth to everyone but you?"

Eli turns back to me after opening his car door. He seems surprised by my question but gives me his version of an answer.

"It's never too late to fight, little one. Now get your ass in this car," he tells me, jerking his head toward the passenger side of his car. "Jace's brother is going to tow your car up to the house."

Climbing into the car with a stranger never felt so safe...

8

SPENCER

I hate customs. At least I wasn't dumb like Stan, trying to bring snacks through in his carry on luggage. I did the smart thing and shipped them home. Did it cost money I really shouldn't be spending? Yes. Will I actually get to have them and not get them confiscated by a hangry TSA agent? Absolutely.

Although, there's no guarantee that Toby and Shiloh won't get curious and open the box before I get home. I tried to plan it so the delivery would arrive after I do, but there's no guarantee.

"Do you have anything to declare?" the tired woman asks me. I answer "No" and get my stamp and go on about my day. Stan has been there for twenty minutes declaring everything and making the agent's day miserable. He's finally cut loose after another minute, and immediately starts complaining that they confiscated things from him.

"I told you to ship the food stuff," I say as we start

walking through the airport trying to find our gates. "You did this to yourself. Now, you don't have time to have a decent meal with your newest bestie before we are tragically separated by fate."

I throw the back of my hand against my forehead in my most dramatic damsel pose and laugh when he shoves me to get me moving again. I hate to say it, but I am going to miss the guy. He's definitely not a little, like I want in my life, but I've been around him enough to say he's a strong contender for a middle. He needs a guide, not a keeper. I'm a full-time Daddy, but for Stan I've adopted a kind of big brother role.

"I still say you should abandon that small fry city and come to the A.T.L.," he mutters as we reach his gate first. "I got way too used to you keeping me on track this month. My mom got used to the regular calls."

I laugh because it's kind of true. His mother wanted a call every day. The surprise and joy in her voice on the fourth day was hilarious to me. I was included in the calls most days purely because I stayed in the room. It was selfish of me, but I miss having a mother's love. Having Mrs. Sinclair essentially adopt me over the course of the program was a wonderful side effect of getting Stan as a roommate.

"At least now, you'll be in the same city and she can come find you to beat some sense into you when you forget," I remind him, pushing him to the gate since his flight just started boarding. "Text me when you land, dude."

"Yes, Dad," he says with a huff. I chuckle because he

knows what I'm into. He found out I was a Daddy the first night when I was getting on him to pick up after himself. The look of surprise on his face when he realized was priceless.

Once Stan is out of sight, I head for my own gate. I have about an hour before boarding will start, so I power on my cell phone to check my messages. I say a prayer of thanks to the heavens that I put my phone on silent before turning it off because Holy Toledo, there are a lot of messages. The group chat for the house is going insane.

> **Eric:**
> So is the cutie joining us?

> **Toby:**
> I dunno. Eli kicked us out of the bar.

> **Shiloh:**
> He seems sad

> **Me:**
> What's going on? What cutie?

For Eli to close the bar at barely ten on a Thursday night means something serious. As one of the three resident Doms of Kink Manor, I have a need to know what happened to make him shut down early.

> **Toby:**
> DADDY SPENCE! Just the man we need!

Scott:
Down, puppy!

Let Eli chime in before you get your hopes up.

Jace:
Do you think he forgives me for scaring him?

Scott:
Of course, TB. He knows you didn't mean it.

Toby:
But seriously…Spence, remember that party?

Eli:
Tobias! Knock it off!

KM-We have a stray for the night

Maybe longer

I chuckle at the string of happy emojis that go on for the next minute. If Eli is the one bringing home a stray, they must be in bad shape. But there isn't any other group of guys out there that I would ever trust to help as much as the ones I share a house with.

"We are now starting the boarding process for flight nineteen twenty two to Pittsburgh at gate ..."

Me:
They just called for boarding. I'll see you guys in the morning.

Eric:
You need a pick up?

Me:
Nah, get some sleep after your set.

I'll catch a rideshare

Jay:
Just woke up. Lemme catch up

Me:
Gotta go

Jay:
Save your money S

I'll grab you from the airport. I'm off tonight.

Me:
OK I'll text when I land

Jay:
I'll be in the area. Might drive a bit for some book funds.

Me:

Toby:
Seriously Spence...

Eli:
Enough, Tobias! Leave it!

Lucky doesn't remember that night as a good thing.

ADMIN ELI HAS SET AN EVENT: House Meeting – Friday 10am

There is a pit in my stomach after those last few messages from Eli. Who is this Lucky person and why am I dreading this house meeting?

9

SPENCER

Three in the morning on a Friday is basically abandoned at the Pittsburgh airport. Just for curiosity's sake, I open up the rideshare app to see what the cost of a ride would be, and there are zero cars in the area. Like, the app is telling me that my wait time would be forty-five minutes, so I'm even more thankful to Jay for coming to pick me up at this hour.

Think of the devil and he shall appear...

"Well hello, my favorite vampire Dom," I call out to him as he gets out to help load all of my crap into his PT Cruiser. I don't know how he manages it, but his car is immaculate on the outside and under the hood. The interior is gaudy as all hell, but clean. If I didn't know better, I might actually believe the man truly is a vampire. Purple velvet does not need to be lining the doors or under my ass in a car.

"Did you have this much shit when you left?" he asks

as he hefts the second of three trunks into the back of the car. "I can tetris like a mother fucker, but seriously?"

"If we could fit all of Toby's puppy gear plus his dorm room into the back of this thing, I am pretty sure there isn't going to be a problem fitting my camera gear and a couple of suitcases," I tell him as I load the last trunk and he shoves my last suitcase on top. "Plus, you know you like a tight fit."

The security guy standing outside of the baggage claim doors starts choking in response to my quip, and the two of us break into laughter as we climb into the front of the Cruiser. Jay puts on his typical early aughts emo music while I settle in for the ride. We are going to have a house meeting in under seven hours, and I'm already short on sleep from the multiple flights. At least Jay works nights, so he's used to being awake at this time.

"Before you crash," he says making me sit up straighter and look at him. "What do you think about this Lucky guy?"

I look at Jay in utter confusion. I have been on another continent for the last fucking month, and on planes for the last day. How in the fuck would I know anything about him? I say as much to my completely idiotic friend and driver, and he chuckles in response.

"Figured I would ask since the pup said you guys met before," he tells me as he merges onto the abandoned parkway. "Something about blood and a party and the guy passing out in your room... I only got bits and pieces while I was waiting for my coffee to brew."

It takes me a few minutes to remember what Toby could possibly have been talking about, but the memory finally comes. It was spring semester sophomore year, the post-midterm bash thrown by the Thetas.

"Come on, Spenceroni!" Big Brother Adam keeps calling me down to join the craziness. The only reason I even pledged Phi Theta Gamma is because my dad was a Theta. Being a legacy meant that I wouldn't have to deal with the pledge pranks and all that crap. It was a guaranteed in with a group of guys who would hopefully one day help me with networking when I manage to launch my photography business.

Instead of the business minded future titans of industry, I ended up with the dumbest group of coochie-obsessed fuck-nuggets that ever existed. The party just started an hour ago and I've already prevented three fires, and two public urinations. I am so not cut out for life in the house...

"Spenceroo! Don't make me come up and get you... FUCK!"

The sound of breaking glass has me bolting for the stairs. Looking down, I see Adam with his shirt off and wrapped around his hand which is now bleeding. The mirror at the base of the steps has a decidedly Adam-shaped crackling in the center with a few shards missing. I can only assume they are either on the ground or in the dumbass's bleeding hand.

"Go get the first aid kit under the sink," I yell down in frustration, and he staggers off into the other room. The

man is three years older than I am and in graduate school. Why the hell am I taking care of his ass?

When I get to the bottom of the stairs, I notice a smaller guy leaning heavily against the banister, looking on the verge of a panic attack. "You alright?" I ask him, Adam forgotten for the time being. I'd rather take care of this adorable guy instead of the asshole who is singlehandedly responsible for every repair bill needing to be paid out on the house before the year ends.

The guy shakes his head and reaches up to grab the handrail in a white-knuckle grip.

"The blood," he whispers. I can barely hear him over the music pumping out of the speakers. "Going down..."

His knees give out and I catch him. I'm tempted to pick him up and carry him. He's small enough... the perfect size for me. But I don't want to put that kind of attention on him since no one has shown any interest in our exchange so far. I wouldn't care, but until I can have a discussion with him, I don't want to risk him feeling like I'm belittling him or anything. Most guys don't appreciate being "babied." Unfortunately, for me, that is exactly the kind of guy that I want...

I put my arm around his tiny waist to keep him upright, throwing his arm over my shoulders. He manages to stay semi-conscious long enough to get him to my bedroom. When he hits the bed, the chocolate curls on his head fall into his face and he pulls my pillow into his arms, like a stuffie.

Oh, this guy is a fucking wet dream.

I reach to brush the curls out of his eyes, but Adam's

belligerent shouting makes me pause before my fingers can make contact. As much as I want to know how soft those curls are, the asshole will likely burn the place down if someone isn't watching him.

"Rest well, little bit," I whisper to the boy in my bed as I pull a blanket over him. "I'll be back soon."

When I finally make it back up to the room, he is gone. The only sign to let me know I didn't imagine him is the neatly folded blanket at the foot of the bed. I never make my bed...

"Good boy," I whisper to the night, hoping somehow someday I will meet him again.

If the stray that Eli brought home is my boy from the party, I will thank every deity in existence. After that night, I searched campus high and low for the guy. I thought I saw him a couple of times near the freshman dorms, but by the time I would get over there, he was gone. At the end of the semester, I swore I would find him in the fall, but he wasn't there.

If this guy coming into the manor is indeed the guy from the party, I want to know what happened. I want to know why he left... I want to know if I made any impact on him at all that night.

Who am I kidding? The guy was barely conscious when I helped him into my bed and didn't see me again. He hadn't seen me before or after. There is no way he knows who I am.

When we pull up to the house, Jay surprises me by

leaving everything packed in the car. He hates leaving tasks unfinished even worse than I do.

In response to my look he says, "Let Jace feel helpful in the morning. He's having a bad time of it after Lucky's first encounter with him."

Jace is a *big* guy. He's almost seven foot tall and even though he's got no body fat on him, he weighs in at over three hundred fifty pounds. The man looks like he should be a professional wrestler or leading a motorcycle gang, but on the inside he is an insecure little boy who just wants to cuddle everything cute. We all decided to surprise him with his very own kitten on his twenty third birthday this November, but based on the way Jay is talking, maybe we should move that up.

"What happened when they met?" I ask as we take off our shoes in the foyer area. Scott is meticulous about shoes in the house, something that some of the former roommates didn't quite understand... hence the former part of that equation. I can't help but notice an unfamiliar pair of Chuck Taylor high tops on the shoe rack. They appear to be custom made with various anime characters featured.

Jay notices as well, even picking one up to examine more closely.

"Guy's got some good taste," he mutters as he turns the shoe side to side. "He's got some obscure ones featured on here, not just the Shonen mainstream stuff."

If there's one thing Jay will have an opinion on, it's anything related to books. Literature, comics, manga, or the smut that everyone's mom reads but swears she doesn't... Jay consumes it all. He even jumped in on the social media influencer thing kind of by accident. He did some sarcastic book reviews on his YouTube channel to piss off an ex-girlfriend and the authors and publishers loved it for some reason. He went viral, and now he gets at least twenty books sent to his PO Box each month in the hopes he will review them. Even the books he dislikes have ended up best sellers, and he hates that most of all.

"Hey guys," Eli whispers as he comes out from within the house to meet us. "Lucky is sleeping on the couch in the parlor. He damn near had another panic attack when he found out that one of us would be giving up a bed to him for the night."

Eli looks worried over this guy. The only person Eli worries about his mom. Between this and hearing Jace is upset, I'm regretting not taking an earlier flight home. Maybe if I had been here, everyone wouldn't be so worked up.

"Don't even go there, Spence," Jay says, giving me a smack upside my head. "I wasn't there either, but from what everyone has said, the guy is strung tighter than Toby got himself when he thought he could do self-bondage with panty-hose last year."

Eli and I both chuckle at the reference, remembering the subsequent trip to the emergency room for stitches when the genius convinced Shiloh to cut him out using a steak knife.

"We're lucky it was only twelve stitches," Eli mutters with a smile.

I reply with, "We're lucky it was Shiloh and not Eric wielding the knife."

Jay slaps his hand over his mouth to hold in his laughter. The man can sleep through anything, but a belly laugh from him will wake the dead. That's the real reason why he has the only soundproofed room in the house, here on the first floor with no one around him. It means he won't disturb us at night when the rest of us are all asleep.

Eli shoots him a look of gratitude and leads the way for us to head into the kitchen. Glancing into the parlor on the way past, all I can see is the top of a head with closely cropped brown hair, and a bright green sock sticking out of each end of the blanket. The Daddy in me wants to go in to cover his foot, but I don't want to chance waking him. If Eli is being this careful over him, he must be in a pretty bad way.

10

After Eli finishes relaying the events of the encounter at the bar, I can understand why our resident teddy bear is worried that he upset our visitor. Based on what Eli said about Lucky's reaction to the blood, I think it might be the guy I remember. If it is my party boy, his fainting can be pretty frightening if you don't know what is happening. He told me what the issue was that night, and I was still freaked out.

Jay and I are sitting on the front porch, waiting for the sun to come up, when Eric pulls up with his typical music blasting. It is almost six in the morning, but the man is full of energy as he climbs down from the cab of his truck.

If it wasn't for the hill we drive up to get to the house, he would still be driving his Fiat every day. Getting stuck at the bottom thanks to the snow last year convinced him to invest in something bigger. Of course, he made the logical leap and got the biggest used truck he could afford. I'm pretty sure it used to be a work truck for Carlisle Construction. If you squint, you can almost see where the decals were ripped away. I would have told him to give it back if Jace's brother hadn't looked it over and given it the okay. The Carlisle family aren't to be trusted.

"What's got the grump puss action goin over there Crocodile Dundee?" Eric asks with a horrible impression of an Australian accent. "Missin you some kangaroos already?"

Jay snickers into the beer bottle he's holding before taking a swig. I can only glower at the freshly showered and definitely freshly fucked drag queen. "Mind the noise," I tell him nodding my head toward the window to the parlor. "Lucky is on the couch. And you might want to get that limp checked out. I heard they do stick removal surgeries at low cost at the animal shelter, Bitch."

I shoot him a wink and receive his signature saucy snap in response. It took a long time for Eric to open up enough to the house to show his true self off of the stage. He's got a lot more in common with Sassy than he does with the guy he was pretending to be for so long. I just wish we could find someone to get it through his head that the *real* Eric is welcome to come out any time, not just at the house or McKinley's.

"How's the boy doing?" Eric asks, dropping onto the steps and swiping one of the beers out of the bucket we brought out. "He didn't look so good when I had to skedaddle out of the bar to get to my gig."

I look at Jay and then give a shrug. "We weren't here when Eli brought him home, and he's been asleep since before we got here."

He hums and takes a healthy swig of his beer. The look in his eyes is one that I hadn't seen before. I thought we broke through the secrets with him, but it looks like there's more we don't know about our favorite queen.

"Aside from the fainting at the sight of blood like a damsel wearing a corset in one hundred degree heat, there's something chasing that boy," he says after shaking himself. "He's all alone, and that ain't right."

I can't stop myself from saying it. Blame it on the beer. Blame it on the lack of sleep. Blame it on the overwhelming irresistible urge that was ingrained in me upon birth.

"It ain't right, but I am. I'm Mister Wright."

The two men on the porch with me give the appropriate groans in response to my terrible pun.

"Being a Daddy does not give you a free pass to tell Dad jokes, dude," Jay says as he gets up from his chair. "You guys staying out here or should I hole up in my room until the house meeting?"

Eric and I look at each other and shrug.

"Grab some pretzels or something," I tell him in response. "I don't want to have all this alcohol and no food going into this meeting in a few hours."

"Screw the pretzels," Eric says, laying down completely across the top step of the porch. "Grab the vodka. I have a night to forget. I gotta stop going for the baby gays... they just don't understand that the asshole isn't a vagina."

"So why not just say no to sex for a night?" I ask him while Jay is inside. I know the real answer, even though Eric will never admit to it. "It might do you good to sleep a full night in your own bed."

As expected, he laughs. "Spencer, babe. If I ever turn down sex, check me into a loony bin. This queen needs a steady diet of dick to survive."

11

LUCKY

The voices from outside rouse me from my sleep, but I don't move from under the blanket. I am so embarrassed that these strangers saw me at my absolute worst last night, but it touches something inside that they still opened their home to me. I was afraid that they were going to push the point of me taking a bed last night, but if I kicked someone out of their own bed, I would never be able to sleep.

I was tempted when Shiloh said the one guy's bed would be empty. He was away for some photography program in Australia for a month, but then Scott reminded him that Spencer was flying home last night. That nixed that idea. Bad enough they wanted me to take away a bed from someone I'd not even met, but I couldn't take his bed... especially not after that amount of traveling.

I know sleeping on planes isn't comfortable for someone of my size, and I'm relatively small for a guy.

Five foot seven isn't super short, but I always seem to be surrounded by giants. Jace is a perfect example of what I'm used to. Before Mother made me stop hanging out with them, my cousins all surpassed me in height. Both Gramps and the men on my father's side are over six foot. Mother is the only one in the family that makes me feel tall since she takes after her mother.

Even my wife is taller than I am.

EX... ex-wife.

I have to remember that. That fact is the *only* bright spot in this entire fiasco. I smile even with the tears leaking from my eyes. Well, maybe not the only bright spot. Somehow, I found myself in the company of some amazing guys.

The chuckles coming from outside capture my curiosity enough that I pull the blanket off my head. I am surprised to see that there is light peeking around the outside of the curtains. The room is so dark that I thought it was still nighttime. Pulling out my phone, I power it back on. I had turned it off to conserve the battery since I didn't bother to grab my charger or anything from the car.

I jump up in surprise at the time showing on the screen. I actually managed to sleep a full eight hours. That hasn't happened in years. The shock turns to wariness when my phone starts vibrating like crazy with alerts. I unlock the phone to see who sent me all of the texts, since there are too many to show in the previews. I had only shut it off about nine hours ago. Every text sent was well after I would have been asleep.

> **Wifey:**
> Where the hell are you?

> **Wifey:**
> This phone belongs to me. You have no right to take it.

> **Wifey:**
> You fucking loser. Everything you own is mine.

> **Wifey:**
> By the way, Dad is keeping your last paycheck to cover the expenses for abandoning the job.

I can feel my pulse rising. She fucking took everything from me! Why the fuck can't I keep my phone? My paycheck? She's claiming I own nothing. The judge hasn't even ruled on the assets yet, but she sure is confident that everything is going to be coming down in her favor. I wish I knew where that investigator she found was so I could let him know exactly how much he fucked me over.

> **Wifey:**
> You can't run from me.

> **Wifey:**
> I don't know who gave you money for a car, but you won't get away.

> **Wifey:**
> You think you can go back to school?
> Just wait until they hear what you've
> done.

> **Wifey:**
> Don't you know about the morals
> clause?

Morals clause? Oh, no...

No. No. No... This can't be happening. She can't take this from me, too. She already stole my family and my money. Can't she just let me have my future?

I hit the power button on the phone to turn it off without bothering to look at any other messages that might have come in. Nothing else matters. My life is over. If I can't go back to school, I'll never get a decent job. I'll never be able to set foot in Holloway Industries. Hell, at this point, I'd be lucky if I could get a job at a fast-food restaurant.

Then again, you need an address for an application. Maybe I can use Gramp's address just for the application. It's not like they use it for anything important now in the age of direct deposit and email delivery of paystubs. In the meanwhile, I hope my two hundred dollars is enough to fix whatever the hell is wrong with my car so I have a place to sleep.

Grabbing a throw pillow from the other end of the couch, I bury my face into it and scream.

Why can't she just leave me alone?

12

SPENCER

The entire house is gathered in the kitchen instead of the parlor because our impromptu house guest is still laying in there. I noticed when Jay, Eric, and I were coming in that the door was shut, so I put my ear to it while the others headed to the kitchen to start the coffee the others would no doubt need. It was quiet, but the sounds of crying were unmistakable. The Daddy in me wanted to go in and gather him up in a hug, but my rational side reminded me that he likely has zero clue who I even am at this point.

At my suggestion, Eli went in to check on him and announced via our group chat that the meeting was moved to the kitchen. When I asked him if Lucky was alright, he just said we'd talk in the meeting so that he wouldn't have to repeat himself. I've never seen rage like I saw in his eyes coming out of that room. Eli might be a Sadistic Dom, but he doesn't do well with pain that isn't consensual. Whatever Lucky told him, Eli wants to destroy the person who hurt that boy.

As Jace curls around his cup of creamer with a dash of coffee, Eli taps a spatula against the counter to bring us all to attention. Jay snorts in his attempt to stifle his laugh causing Eli to shrug.

"The bell is in the parlor, so we're improvising," he says with a half-smile. The smile disappears when he continues. "I think Jay and Spence are the only ones who haven't met our houseguest yet, but I'm sure they will agree with me when I say, I don't want him to leave before we take care of whatever brought him to our door."

Heads nod around the room, and Shiloh raises his hand slowly. Our little kitten is still so very skittish, but he's growing more confident by the day. Eli hands him the spatula to signify that the kitty cat has the floor.

"I know I should have used the kitchen upstairs, but I was worried about Lucky being down here all alone," he starts and looks scared that we are going to scold him for using the big kitchen. I walk over and pull the smaller man into my side for a quick squeeze. Shiloh isn't a fan of uninvited touch, but comfort touches like this where he can break away if he wants to are sometimes just what he needs to know we love him.

He exhales and his shoulders drop, releasing some of the tension he had been carrying.

"The door to the parlor was open and he was screaming into a pillow," the young man says quietly. "I didn't understand all of it, but apparently his ex is the problem. He kept saying *"Why can't she just leave me alone? She took everything."* Just that same kind of thing over and over.

"I wanted to give him a comfort cuddle, but I know I wouldn't appreciate a stranger touching me when I'm like that, so I just pulled the door closed for him and went back to my room," he says hanging his head. When he looks back up at us, he asks, "Did I do the right thing? Should I have hugged him?"

"Oh my precious negra gatita, you were purrrrrfect," Eric croons from his perch in the bean bag chair in the corner. He's still half drunk from our sunrise porch party, but the sentiment is appreciated.

"You can't call him a black cat just because he's black," Scott mutters into his coffee cup causing the rest of the room to bust into laughter. Scott is our singular switch in the house, but before coffee he is almost always stuck entirely into his middle mindset. His middle side is a moody pre-teen who rarely shows consideration for others. Last night must have really affected him. I'm sure the stress of having to be the dominant one coming back to the house before Eli got home with Lucky didn't help.

One on one or in a support role, Scott can easily be as dominant as the situation calls for. Having to comfort Jace and Shiloh while reeling in Toby with no help couldn't have been an easy task. Glancing at Eli and Jay, it looks like none of us considered what a toll last night might have taken on more than just Lucky.

Jay grabs the spatula when Shiloh places it back on the island.

"I propose a new house rule," he says, making sure everyone is paying attention. "If there are more than three submissives in a room, and yes Scott I am including you, one of the Doms of the house must be present, especially if someone is upset."

I nod in agreement, but Eli takes the spatula from Jay's hands.

"This will go to a vote," he says looking at each of us in turn. "I'll put the box in the... shit. Can't use the parlor right now..."

"Here on the counter will work," I suggest before one of the subs, Eric or Toby mainly, catches on to the slip in words and suggests the shitter. "We can have dinner at the bar and order pizza to welcome me back. Australian pizza is totally not the same."

Eric jerks awake from the light doze his body is trying to put him in to say, "What? Did you miss all of the dangerous toxins and preservatives?"

"Can't live without 'em," I say with a chuckle.

Eli shakes his head and taps the counter with the spatula to get our attention.

"Back to the reason we're here so some of us can get some sleep," he says. "Lucky needs our help, but he can't stay on the couch forever."

"He can take my room," Shiloh says softly, causing us all to turn to him in surprise. "I'm not sure I like sleeping by myself in my own room. The nightmares came back."

When the man lets out a whimper, Toby pulls him into a hug. The pup is the only one whose touch Shiloh never struggles against. "You know you can always come into my room," he says, rubbing his best friend's back. "I love a good puppy pile with my favorite kitten."

Eli looks at the two of them before glancing my way. I nod to show my agreement. If Shiloh moves in with Toby, that puts Lucky in the other room on the top floor of the house with me. I can keep an eye on him, as well as provide him with the space to find his way in the chaos that Kink Manor really is.

There is a separate lounge area up there as well as a kitchenette. The bathroom is only a shower and toilet, but at least it looks like he's short enough to be able to use the shower. I go down to the second floor because my six foot four ass has to hunch to even fit under the slanted ceiling in that glorified closet, let alone get into a position where the water will get me clean.

"I'll help him move in whatever stuff he needs to," I say. "Jackson dropped off his car around seven this morning. It doesn't look like he has much."

"He didn't come in?" Jace asks in a sad voice. He loves his older brother to a fault, but Jackson is still trying to break Jace of the codependency they developed in the foster care system. Although not blood related, they were adopted by the same couple and given new names when they were twelve and fourteen.

"Not today, Teddy Bear," I tell him. "He had to get to work but wanted to help us get Lucky's car off the side of the highway and up the hill. You know Steve would have charged him."

I watch the hurt drain out of the big man and for the millionth time curse the man who calls himself his brother. I don't know what happened to make Jackson think he has to stay away, but our giant teddy bear deserves to have someone firmly in his corner, not this wishy-washy bullshit.

"I'll check in with him later to make sure Lucky doesn't get a bill," Eli says to reassure the big man. "Now that we've addressed where Lucky will be sleeping starting tonight, we have to take care of the other elephant in the room. Stress levels have been a bit too high lately and we're about to run into more responsibilities with the new semester starting soon, so who is up for a field trip to the Devil's Club?"

Every hand raises in the room, but our attention gets pulled to the hallway by a knock against the door frame. I turn around, only to see a ghost from mere months ago.

Why is Sabrina Carlisle's husband in our house?

"Sorry to interrupt your meeting but can someone tell me where the bathroom is again?" he asks while pointedly not looking at anyone. "I only remember about the one downstairs in the basement, but I don't want to cut through your meeting or wander around your house looking for myself."

While Shiloh takes our guest upstairs, I pour through my memories of the man I investigated. It was a chore to stay away from him each time I was near him. Everything about what he was doing at that motel screamed that he is a little in need of a Daddy or Mommy, but he is married. Having him here in this house is going to be a test of my self control...

I am so fucking screwed.

13

LUCKY

After Shiloh took me up to the second floor to use the bathroom, I expected him to lead me back down to the room they let me sleep in last night. Instead, he grabbed my hand to lead me up to the top level of the house. He asked me to start pulling his clothes out of the closet and left me alone in his room while he ran downstairs to get something.

I am so confused, but it feels nice to not have to think and just have something to do. Helping the quiet man reorganize his clothing is something I can handle. Sabrina didn't let me touch her clothing. Hell, she barely let me touch my own. My clothes for each day were hung on my door each morning like she thought me incapable of dressing myself, like I haven't been doing it for most of my life. After being treated like shit for the last year, I'm happy to be allowed to just exist.

Shiloh comes back into the room with some boxes to

put the clothing in, so I pull the items off the hangers and fold them neatly to go into the boxes.

"You don't have to fold them," he says, grabbing a shirt from the closet and just throwing it into a box, hanger and all. I can't repress my shudder. "They're just going downstairs to get hung up again in Toby's room. I just don't want to drag them and get them dirty."

I shake my head frantically at him. "But they'll get wrinkled if you just throw them in a box, even for a short trip. Then you'll have to iron them, maybe even another wash. That's wasting energy. That's more money for bills. That's less money for other things, important things, like pizza and chocolate and..."

I can feel myself hyperventilating. I haven't had a panic attack triggered by cleaning in a while. It is usually my happy place, but after the last few days, my stress levels are too high. The thought of intentionally allowing a mess to happen. Sabrina used to do that... make a mess to force me to clean it up over and over again. The memories start to assault me. It's too much.

I grab at my hair, but there isn't enough there to grab. Sabrina made me cut off my hair... said it wasn't right for a grown man to have curly hair. Without my hair to pull, I start to drag my nails up and down my arms. The sensation will eventually ground me... usually before drawing blood, but not always. Part of me *wants* to bleed now. At least then, I can pass out and escape. At least then, I'm not an embarrassment who can't handle not folding a damn shirt.

"SPENCER!"

Shiloh's voice sounds very far away even though he's less than two feet from me. He sounds scared. Am I scaring him?

Just great. Another thing that I'm a total fuckup at.

Strong hands grab my wrists, but I have to do something. I squirm, trying to break free, but the hands are like iron cuffs. There is no give to them.

"Shhhh, little one," a deep voice commands me. "You need to calm down. Everything will be alright. Just settle."

His words wash over me, but I still can't concentrate. The shirt is still just sitting in the box. I need to fold it before it sets. I need to fix it.

"Little one, what is it about the box that is bothering you?" the voice asks and I have to answer.

"The shirt. It's going to be wrinkled. It can't be wrinkled," I tell him on a whimper. "It can't be wrinkled. She won't stop if it's wrinkled. I have to get her to stop."

I hold my breath as I watch Scott pull out the shirt to remove the hanger and fold it. He does a good enough job that my anxiety starts to calm a bit and I feel like I can at least breathe again. I watch his movements while he proceeds to finish the pile I started and takes the boxes out of the room. From the top of the stairs, I hear him say, "I'll get the rest when you're done talking."

Talking? Who is talking? I look around before the tug on my wrists reminds me that I'm not alone in the room. I look up into the face of Mr. Deep Voice only to recognize the man who led me to the room in the frat house... the man who helped set me up for almost two full years of hell.

I see the moment he realizes I recognize him. The guilt is plain on his face.

"She was right," I whisper. "I'll never get away."

I tear my wrists from his grip and pound down the stairs, my tears blinding me as I make my way to escape. I can't stay here another second. This was all a set-up. I'll never be free...

I ignore the men yelling at me. It doesn't matter. They'll never see me again anyways.

She's right. I'll never escape... not while I'm alive.

I grab my shoes and launch myself off the porch. I know I'm ruining my socks, but I can't stop. My feet carry me forward, running for the woods. I'll lose them in the trees. Gramps taught me all about how to hide my trail. I'll just circle back after they give up to grab my bag and then Lucas Anthony Holloway will disappear completely.

14

SPENCER

I call after the boy who just ran from me. He's really fast, too fast to catch up. By the time I reach the porch, he is already entering the woods. Eli and the others pour out of the house behind me, Jay in his pajamas. I guess he hasn't gone to bed yet.

"What the fuck, Spence?" Jay asks, staring at the tree line. "What the fuck did you do?"

I can't look away from the trees to say anything in response, but Shiloh takes it upon himself to take the blame.

"It's my fault," he whimpers before running back into the house. Toby shoots me a questioning glance before running after his friend. The others on the porch all look at me with varying levels of accusation, but Scott is the only one to speak up.

"When I left the room, he was calming down," he says, moving into my direct line of sight and forcing me to look away from the woods. "What changed?"

I stagger backwards until my back makes contact with the pillar and glance back at the trees.

"He recognized me," I say and fight to hold my emotions in check.

"And that is a problem, why?" asks Eric, obviously grumpy now that his buzz is wearing off. "Why would that cutie pie recognizing you cause a reaction like this? I fucking ran because of you! You understand how pissed off I am right now that you made me run, right?"

Eli shakes his head in amusement at Eric's remark, but levels me with a serious glare.

"We need the story, Spence," he says to me. "If we're going to be his safe haven, I need to know if there is an issue with him staying here. If I have to, I can call the landlord about one of the trailers. I can even try and set him up with a friend in another city. No matter what, there's something here that isn't making sense."

"Toby said you met him at a Theta party last year?" Scott prompts to get the conversation started.

I nod my head and pick up the story. "It was the my sophomore year, so not this past year, but right before I moved in here.

"That's where I met him, but I doubt that's where he knows me from," I say. "He was practically unconscious when I came across him. I basically carried him to my bedroom and tucked him in when that dumbass Adam started bleeding in front of him."

The guys still out on the porch all nod their heads in understanding, having knowledge of Lucky's response to blood. They don't know the rest of the story though.

"But the real issue is from just a few months ago. Remember how I had to take a case kind of last minute to pay for the program?" I ask and again get a round of nods in affirmation.

"Well, Lucky was kind of that case."

15

SPENCER

"We are definitely going to need more than that," Jay says before pushing Jace back toward the door. "But we are going to need coffee first. I have a feeling it is going to be a very long conversation, or very tense...Maybe both. Either way, coffee."

With a chuckle, Eli follows. Scott heads inside right after Eli, but Eric stays to watch me.

"Did you know?" Eric asks me, and I just stare at him. That question is a loaded one and can refer to a lot. "Did you know he was your last case?"

Out of all of the housemates, only Eric knew how much it bothered me to take a case from Sabrina Carlisle. He was a year ahead of us in school, and part of a rich family, so he is familiar with her tactics. While I was working the case, we spent most of the time I was back here at the house coming up with ideas to help her husband get away from her. Never in a million years did I think I would have that man in my house, in my arms.

At my shrug, he snaps at me. "Either you knew or you didn't Spencer! Did you know that Lucky Hollow was your last case?!"

"Wait, Hollow?" I ask. The name is tripping me up. That wasn't the name Sabrina gave me. Actually, come to think of it... "She said her husband's name was Lucas. I figured since she didn't change her name, he must have changed his to match hers. I mean he was even working for Carlisle Construction and all. I never even checked since the motel was a cash only transaction."

Of course, Jay and Eli chose that moment to come back outside with two extra cups of coffee for us.

"So you're saying the Carlisle cheating case was for *Lucky*?" Eli asks incredulously. "That boy can't lie to save his life. How in the hell would he have the guts to cheat on someone like Sabrina Carlisle?"

I shake my head at him before taking a sip. "He didn't cheat on her," I tell them, glancing back toward the trees. I'm hoping he'll come back after he calms down. He can't get anywhere without a car or his stuff.

"Uh, dude," Eric says holding up his phone, "According to this, he did."

<u>Holloway Heir Exposed.</u>
<u>Wife Abandoned for Cheap Trysts.</u>
<u>Exclusive Interview</u>
<u>with Sabrina Carlisle-Holloway</u>

I snatch the phone out of his hand and start reading:

Every girl wants to be a princess, but how often do we see what happens after the wedding bells stop ringing? Cinderella supposedly got her happily ever after, but who is to say that Prince Charming didn't step out on her? Our team sat down with the newly divorced Sabrina Carlise, ex-wife of the disgraced Lucas Anthony Holloway, former heir to Holloway Industries.

Staff: Ms. Carlisle, how did you discover your husband was being unfaithful?

Sabrina: Well, to be honest, I didn't want to believe it was possible. With how much Mrs. Holloway, my mother-in-law, preaches of the importance of fidelity, I initially dismissed it when James, his former roommate, brought it to my attention.

Staff: So, you didn't catch him directly?

Sabrina: No, unfortunately. He lied every time, saying he had business meetings with clients to help expand my father's construction company.

Staff: What happened after James told you?

Sabrina: At first, I didn't want to believe it, you know? I swore till death do us part, but apparently it didn't mean the same to him. I should have paid closer attention to the pre-nup he forced me to sign, but I was in love.

Staff: Tell us more about this pre-nuptial agreement.

Sabrina: It basically said that if we divorce or he dies, I would get nothing. It was incentive to stay married to him, but I just couldn't take the lies anymore.

Staff: With such an agreement in place, how did you get the judge to rule in your favor?

Sabrina: James convinced me to get a private investigator to get proof of the infidelity, so I tried for weeks to get someone to listen to me, to go up against a powerhouse family name like the Holloways. Finally, an old elementary school friend offered his help. He got me the proof I needed to get the judge to see the truth.

Staff: Can we include these photos in the article? Are they protected by any privileges?

Sabrina: I've consulted my lawyer and he told me that I'm free to share the photographs since they were taken in a public space and the photographer, my friend, handed them over willingly.

Staff: What happened after the judge ruled in your favor?

Sabrina: Lucas just disappeared. He somehow managed to empty out our bank account and took off for God only knows where. Then, my father called me to let me know he had done the same with Carlisle Construction. Lucas Holloway embezzled millions, stole hundreds of thousands of dollars from his family, and disappeared. No one has seen him since he bought a used car and left the city two days ago.

Staff: Do you regret getting involved with him?

Sabrina: I made a mistake sleeping with him when he pressured me at a fraternity party my sophomore year of college. That night resulted in a pregnancy where he used his money to convince me to keep the baby. His mother forced us to marry, while his father forced the pre-nup. After we were married he drank to the point of abusiveness. I lost the baby because of his addiction.

Staff: Are you pressing charges against your ex-husband?

Sabrina: I just want to know he is safe. As for any charges, that is up to the police investigating the matter.

Staff: Thank you for your time today, Ms. Carlisle and we wish you well in your future. With luck, you will find a man who is truly worthy of you.

Please see below for the photographs provided to our studio. More on this story as it develops. Video at six.

For more information on the upheaval at Holloway Industries, please see the press release from this morning

Holloway Industries Blacklists Heir:

College Dropout Lucas Holloway Denied Employment After Divorce

I open the file with the photos, and I'm blown away. Some of the photos are the ones that I took, but there are at least three that are obviously from another camera and day. The lighting is wrong, and the person taking the photo doesn't understand how to actually capture someone's appearance. There was never a woman at the motel, and these photos don't show anything except a blond woman standing at the door of the room Lucky was in the night I took his photos.

"I'm going to fucking kill her," I growl out. The last photo of the woman is clearly Sabrina in a wig based on the reflection off the car window.

Eric manages to snatch his phone out of my hand before I throw it, but my anger isn't subsiding. Eric passes the phone to Eli so that he and Jay can read the article while I pace the porch in my rage. *How dare she use my photos to frame him!* The man I observed wanted nothing more than some junk food and cartoons, but she painted him as not only a liar and a cheater, but a thief as well.

Eli pulls out his own phone and starts sending a message to God only knows who. When he glances up, there is a feral look in his eye.

"Let's see how the bitch likes the media turned against her," he says. "Spencer, it's time to brush the dust off and get a *real* investigation going."

His phone pings and his smile widens. "You've just been officially hired to investigate Sabrina Carlisle and her false claims against one Lucas Anthony Holloway aka Lucky Hollow. You have an unlimited budget, and your fee deposit is half a million dollars."

I choke on my coffee... Half a what now?

Jay whistles before he takes a sip from his own mug. "His parents?" he asks after a minute.

"Nope," Eli says, popping the P with a chuckle. "Our landlord."

16

LUCKY

They didn't even chase me off the porch. I ran deeper into the woods for about five minutes before I realized I didn't hear any footsteps following me. Without someone chasing me, I don't see a point in running, so I turn around to trek back toward the house after putting my shoes on. It doesn't take long to find the trail back, but at the edge of the tree line, I decide to stay hidden. Instead of sitting and waiting for the coast to clear, I creep along in the shadows to get close enough to listen to the guys talking on the porch.

Crouching down behind a bush, I stay as still and quiet as possible.

"Our landlord?" Eric asks. I can't see who the question is directed to, but Eli is the one who answers.

"He is very interested in the well-being of everyone who is invited to live in the manor," Eli says. "He already gave his blessing for Lucky to move in, so he's one of us now."

I'm one of them? Someone who has never even met me, wants me when my own family has rejected me. This mysterious landlord wants me here and is even willing to protect me...Honestly sounds too good to be true, but they don't know I'm listening. It must be true. But why?

"Can you get a press release to counter the interview before the video airs?" I'm guessing that one was Spencer. I never got an actual introduction between him helping my ex-wife set me up with a fake pregnancy and him trying to keep me from running away to save myself.

"It will be tough to get someone to air it, especially without his side of things," Jay says. Whose side are these guys on that they need some man's word. Knowing my luck, they'll paint me as a thief or something so my former father-in-law can get sympathy donations to his failing company. I'm pretty sure if my twenty million couldn't save it, nothing can. But he's welcome to try.

"They can interview me," Spencer says. "I have the original files, my copy of the notarized statement that was supposed to go to the judge, and the notice of receipt that both she and her lawyer received them. Plus, if I have a couple hours, I could probably find out where the money went as well."

I'm so confused about what they could be talking about at this point, so I pull out my phone to look up what might have been happening. The battery shows I'm at about ten percent, but it's enough to open the browser and look up my name. Against my better judgment, I have to see what fresh hell my ex-wife has decided to put me through since I didn't reply to any of her eighty two text messages over the last twelve hours...

17

SPENCER

Avery didn't manage to get my interview aired or printed before six, but that was by design. Eli might be a Sadist, but he also doesn't like to drag things out. His call was to refute Sabrina's interview before her lies could be broadcast, but Eli doesn't know Sabrina Carlisle like Eric and I do. She would have found a way to claim the media twisted her words and had time to come up with something even worse for Lucky. I wanted her on video, as evidence, for the fraud and defamation case I am building against her.

"You sure you want this delayed?" she asks me as they clip the microphone to my shirt. "We can go live immediately following her clip on Channel Two."

My original plan was to do a breaking news segment after the news was over, but a live rebuttal immediately following... that is freaking genius.

"You are amazing, Avery," I lift her hand for a kiss. "I would marry you if you'd have me."

She giggles and uses the same response she always has, "Alas, I'm monogamous and like the D a bit too much to go for a sexless marriage."

The staff around us snort or choke in response to our banter, but we have been friends since middle school. Avery knows Sabrina Carlisle and is one hundred percent on board with the plan to bring her down.

"Alright people! We are going to do a breaking segment as soon as the Carlisle piece ends on the other channels," she announces to the crew around us. "Make sure to have the pictures queued up, and let's make some magic."

Some of the crew cheer, but mostly we are in a waiting game. The monitors at our feet are showing the feeds from the other stations in the area, including the one we are going to be airing on. I look at Avery, and she shrugs.

"Don't blame me," she says. "It would be way too suspicious if we were the only station *not* to air her interview. Plus, you have to admit there's a sense of poetic justice having the anchors intro her interview only to immediately call it out on being bullshit right after."

"You're going to get to that desk before the end of the year," I tell her with a chuckle.

Avery just adjusts her hair and looks at the camera. "Showtime," she whispers and pastes a huge fake smile on her face.

18

LUCKY

I'm a dead man...

Sabrina not only painted me as an adulterer, she announced to the entire city that I stole *my own money* and made it seem like it was a crime... not that I actually have any of the money. She took all of it. Between her and her family, the money is gone. I don't even have the two hundred anymore since I can't even risk going back to the car.

Add onto it the fact that my father's company released a statement that basically makes me unemployable to any company in this region... I'm fucked.

My only hope right now is to find my way to Gramps and hope he will take me in. I can't stay here...

"Anybody seen Lucky come back?" Eli asks as he comes out on the porch. The guys gathered there tell him no, obviously since I haven't gone back yet. "It's getting dark and I'm getting worried."

"Shouldn't you be opening McKinley's by now?" Toby asks.

"Ash is going to work tonight. She's been asking for more hours, anyways," Eli responds as he jumps down from the porch. "We need two people to stay here while the rest of us go check the woods for Lucky. He should have been back to at least grab his stuff by now."

Well, he's not wrong. I should have grabbed my backpack with my wallet at least, but I know they would stop me. It wouldn't take much. I almost came out of hiding when I heard Shiloh's sniffles, but Eric's voice stopped me. He was part of *that* conversation, and I still don't know what side they're coming down on.

"Jay, you and Eric got the least amount of sleep aside from Spencer. Why don't the two of you stay here and wait for him to get back. You can trade off naps if you need to."

"I'm good to go, Boss-man. Don't need no stinking naps." Eric's voice is trying to hard to be Miss Sassy, but it falls flat. There's a heaviness to him and it's all my fault.

But I don't know who to trust...

While they argue over who is coming into the woods after me, I start to move in the direction I think the road is. I can at least get a head start and lose them completely once the sun goes down. Being in the woods has always been one of my favorite things, but I need to get away from them so that I can think things through. Losing the sun means I'm temporarily losing my sense of direction, at least until the stars really get to shine. There's not as much light pollution here, but the canopy is thick, so I'm going to have to rely on other ways to tell where I'm heading.

19

SPENCER

"In the age of misinformation and he said she said games, we are often left in the situation of having to decipher for ourselves what the truth is. A wise person once said there are three versions of events. Person A remembers things one way. Person B remembers things a different way. The truth is somewhere in between.

"Now, as nice as this idea is when it comes to recollecting events, it does not refute hard evidence or excuse defamation, fraud, or blatant falsification of evidence. Today, we have with us the very same investigator whose photographs were used by Ms. Carlisle to convince a judge to grant her a divorce on the grounds of infidelity.

"I am pleased to introduce Mr. Spencer Wright of Mr. Wright Investigations. Tell me, Spencer, why come forward today? Why not set things straight at the hearing with the judge?"

I glare at Avery since she knows this was not the planned script for the interview. I was supposed to show the photos and the notarized report and that was supposed to be it. She's trying to turn this into a prime-time special... Now, I remember why we don't hang out more.

"I didn't even know the hearing was scheduled," I tell her. "Usually, the time between when I give my report to a client to the time a hearing reaches a judge is at least three months. I've been called as late as two years after filing my report.

"As for the Carlisle case, I submitted my report to the client, Ms. Sabrina Carlisle, on July thirteenth before boarding a plane for Australia on the sixteenth. I spent the last month in a cultural exchange program through my school and only returned yesterday. I received no notice of a subpoena or summons to appear at neither my office, nor my home address, both of which are readily available on the report I provide to my clients for that very purpose."

Avery knows all of this because she has hired me herself before to help find her sister and get her away from an abusive boyfriend. The smile on her face is devious, but it fits when she asks, "So are you saying that Ms. Carlisle purposefully didn't have you called to court, even after using your photographs?"

I know what my friend is up to. She's setting me up to blow it all out of the water. I told her how I already feel about Lucky. She knows what I'm looking for, what I want. She also knows just how much I've obsessed over the boy from the party.

"I've read the court transcripts. The lawyer for Mr.

Holloway attempted to send a summons multiple times, but the address he was provided by both Ms. Carlisle's attorney and the agency that records the investigator licenses was not valid. The address he was given was for the Phi Theta Gamma house at the university, where I have not resided in over a year and a half, and was never my address of record as an investigator."

"Couldn't they just use google to find your address?" Avery asks, looking genuinely confused. Before I understood the process in the courtroom, I would have said the same thing.

"Not usually," I answer. "Anyone can build a website these days and make it look legitimate. There is nothing stopping a person from creating a website showing John Smith with an office at twenty two Main Street, but that doesn't mean John Smith actually *has* an office there. The reason the courts need to use official channels is to prevent unrelated persons from being harassed by the courts.

"My fraternity brothers aren't going to be in the house for another week, so the notices are probably still there. I haven't gone to check. I don't like to go in without one of the active residents present. Common courtesy and all."

Avery pauses and I wonder if she is re-thinking this whole thing. She tucks her hair behind her ear and I realize she is getting instructions on how to proceed.

I take a sip of water to cover the pause and she continues to ask another question.

"So what you are saying is either the court official

purposely went to the wrong address or the agency that is paid by the government to keep accurate records for the court has inaccurate information?"

I give her the look that question deserves before answering it.

"What I am saying, is that whether or not I received the summons, it shouldn't have mattered. The evidence I provided Ms. Carlisle proved that her husband was *not* having an affair.

"Mr. Holloway was indeed travelling to a motel twice a month. He would pay for a room and disappear inside for on average three hours each time, but he wasn't meeting anyone or having any type of sexual interaction with anyone."

I didn't share the details of this part of the story with Avery beforehand. Here's the payback for springing unexpected questions on me earlier. The smile on my face must be smug when she inevitably asks, "What *was* Mr. Holloway doing that he had to go through all of this secrecy?"

I take great pleasure in throwing her a smirk before I reply, "He was eating pepperoni pizza and rocky road ice cream while watching cartoons in comfortable pajamas."

There is a bit of perverse joy at the sight of Avery's left eye starting to twitch. It is so much more than just having the wrong parts that kept me and her from falling into bed together. We are basically siblings with the way we go at each other. I don't even try to mask my chuckle before I continue.

"Ms. Carlisle kept a registered dietician and professional chef in the house with orders to throw out anything not approved by her. Mr. Holloway had to sneak off to a roadside motel to enjoy the television and food he enjoyed, instead of being able to relax in his own home.

"The photographs showing this were provided to Ms. Carlisle, but I notice they were missing from her exclusive interview and the court records, along with my report of findings that Mr. Holloway was *not* having an affair.

"I brought them with me today, along with a copy of the notarized receipt that both Ms. Carlisle and her attorney signed upon receipt of my report and the photographs."

Avery's smile is wicked as she looks at the camera and says, "Let's take a look." This damn woman looks like those nineties talk show hosts revealing baby mama drama. If it wasn't for Lucky and my need to fix the mistake I made by taking the damn case, I would never subject myself to this.

We go through each photograph and share a few chuckles when the one photo shows complete devastation on Lucky's face when he dropped his pizza trying to take everything into the room in a single trip. Even the crew laughs at the next photo that showed Lucky scraping the cheese and pepperoni off the pizza box lid. It is a great way to show that he is just a regular guy and not the devious asshole Sabrina tried to paint him as.

After going through all of the photographs I provide, Avery signals for another group to be put up on the screen. "And what about these ones?" she asks when the added photos come up on the monitor.

"These photographs were *not* taken by me, nor are they even the same day as any of the other photographs that show Mr. Holloway at the motel," I tell her. "In fact, if you look at the reflections in the background, you can see the differences."

We are finally back to where we rehearsed. I then go into explaining the technical differences in a way that the average person can understand. That is the reason Avery had me practice this part.

"So basically, Ms. Carlisle took your work, twisted it to fit her narrative, lied to the courts, defamed an upstanding citizen whose only fault was marrying her, and then wasted resources to get her fifteen minutes of fame?"

I know she expects me to just agree and leave it at that, but Sabrina pissed me off. Knowing now, what I wish I knew earlier, I am about to blow the bitch's whole world apart.

"Not only that, Avery," I say and enjoy the way her look of surprise shifts to one of pure joy. "Ms. Carlisle claimed to be impregnated by Mr. Holloway on a night that I know for a fact he was unconscious. If she did have intercourse with him, it was rape on her part. If she lied about the pregnancy, according to the prenuptial agreement that she signed, that is grounds for immediate dissolution of the marriage in addition to the repayment of every cent that Mr. Holloway invested of his personal money into her, their joint property, or any joint business ventures. That includes Carlisle Construction...

"So, is she a rapist or a liar? That is the question that needs to be asked."

Avery is practically bouncing in her seat when she says we need to go to commercial, but we will be right back with more shocking revelations.

"Clear!"

Avery jumps across the set to crush me in a hug. "Spencer! You are singlehandedly launching my career! Please tell me you have something even better than that for after the break?"

I'm smiling as I pull out my phone to check for messages, and the one from Eli wipes the smile from my face.

> **Eli:**
> Heading out to search the woods for Lucky. He hasn't come back for his stuff. I don't want him wandering in the dark.

> We both know how that ridge at the north end of the bowl comes out of nowhere if you don't know it's already there.

> Not to mention the cliff above the DC

> **Me:**
> Enough E! Please don't make me run out on Avery before I finish this. Remember, I'm doing this so that Lucky doesn't have to.

Eli:

I know and I'm sorry. His phone is off
and his family is getting worried.

> **Me:**
>
> His family took the side of his bitch of an
> ex-wife. Let them.

Eli:

Not this member. Not this side. They
actually REALLY care about him

Avery starts signaling me to wrap it up. The break is
ending and this interview has to as well. I shoot off one
last text before I shove the phone back in my pocket.

> **Me:**
>
> Find him. I'll be home as soon as I can to
> join the search. Keep Jay and Eric at the
> house. Lucky is more likely to respond if
> one of the other subs is calling for him.

20

SPENCER

"And we're back with Private Investigator, Spencer Wright, as he reveals all of the misinformation that Ms. Sabrina Carlisle used in her attempt to deceive all of us, dragging not only *his* reputation through the mud, but more importantly, the reputation of her recently divorced ex-husband Lucas Holloway.

"Before the break, Mr. Wright revealed the dubious circumstances surrounding the nuptials and what it would mean for Ms. Carlisle. Mr. Wright, have you ever met Mr. Holloway?"

I cock my head wondering where she is going with this but answer truthfully.

"I met the man in question yesterday, after arriving home from Australia. His car had broken down outside of the place where one of my housemates works, and they offered him our couch to sleep on for the night while we got his car towed somewhere it could be fixed."

"Did you know him prior to yesterday?"

"I saw him at a fraternity party once, the one where Ms. Carlisle claimed to be impregnated. But we didn't even have a conversation," I tell her. "Speaking of the pregnancy again, though. Don't you think it's funny how there was never any medical record, except for the appointment for a paternity test that was cancelled?"

"Why was it cancelled?" Avery asks. She is loving this. In high school she used to go around seeking out the latest gossip just to sate her never-ending curiosity. She is one of those rare people that believes in truth above all.

"My source told me that Ms. Carlisle claimed a miscarriage two days before the paternity test appointment. And before you ask, no. I will not reveal my source outside of a court order."

Avery's pout is cute, but I know it is only for the camera. She is fully aware that the medical records I accessed were not given to me legally.

"Unfortunately due to time restraints, we need to wrap this up, but are there any other details about this case you want to reveal?"

My smile is so predatory that it sends a visible shiver through my friend. "I have a lot, but I will say two more things. Number one, Lucas Holloway has never cheated on his wife, but *she* spent thirteen months of their sixteen-month marriage sharing a bed with James Buchanan and Dustin Coventry on a regular basis, alternating between the two men.

"Number two, Carlisle Construction hasn't turned a profit in over fifteen years. The books actually improved in the time that Mr. Holloway was employed by his father-in-law. My research indicates that Mr. Holloway was using his own funds to pay off the settlements and cover the differences in cost of materials to ensure customers were getting the best possible service. In fourteen months, the Carlisle family and business managed to burn through over nineteen million dollars of Mr. Holloway's personal funds, most of which is still unaccounted for at this time. I am waiting to hear back with quotes from forensic accountants for assistance in tracking down all of the money.

"Whatever is left has been frozen by the judge who granted the divorce, pending the result of Ms. Carlisle challenging the pre-nuptial agreement. Mr. Holloway currently has less than two hundred dollars to his name, and only what belongings he could fit inside a 2009 Nissan Versa. Ms. Carlise has all seven cars, the house, and the staff; however, she still decided to launch this slanderous attack against her ex-husband.

"I leave you with this, Avery. Who is the real liar here? Who is the real thief? I think the evidence speaks for itself, and I would love to do a follow-up with you on this after those responsible receive the necessary punishment for their actions."

"Thank you, Mr. Wright for sharing with us this evening. It has been truly enlightening, and you have once again proven why Mr. Wright Investigations is one of the best in the city."

There is silence for a few seconds until someone calls, "And we're out!"

Avery jumps up and does a silly dance, but I don't have time to celebrate. "Hate to cut and run, but there's an emergency back at the house. I gotta get back there."

She stops dancing and her serious face is on, not the one that she shows to people at work or through the camera. This is the real Avery, the true face of my good friend who was there the night my parents were ripped away by a drunk driver.

"Need my help?" she asks. "I'm done for the night, and it won't take me longer than a minute to get out of this suit."

I let out a laugh that I know she expects when she wiggles her eyebrows, but my mind is pushing me to get back as quickly as possible. "I'm going now. You can just show up at the house after you're done changing. Jay and Eric will be there and can show you where you can help."

I run out of the studio as soon as the microphone is unattached from me. My car races home as fast as I reasonably can get there. It's still light out for another forty minutes. I have under an hour to find him before I really will need to test my boy scout skills.

21

LUCKY

Once the sun is gone, the others are easy to spot when they get too close. It's obvious that even though they live surrounded by forest, they don't spend a lot of time in it. They are noisy and using flashlights to navigate. At least, I don't have to worry about giving away my position with one of those. Even if I wanted to use the flashlight, my cell phone is completely dead at this point.

"Lucky? Where are you?"

Eli's voice is so far away, it should be a comfort. But it isn't. My vision blurs as I struggle to keep the warring feelings inside. They wanted me and I ran. Even if they do think I'm a thief and a liar and an adulterer, they want me to be with them. At the very least, I know I can trust Shiloh, Toby, Jace, and Eli... and the mysterious landlord.

I wipe hurriedly at my face and turn to head back toward the house, but in my rush, I miss my footing. Me feeling weightless should only happen on roller coasters, not falling off a cliff. As I tumble through the darkness, the only thought in my head is that I wish I could have told them all I want to be a part of their family, too. I come to an abrupt stop with a thud and a flash of pain radiates up my left arm.

I smell it before I see it. It's like being in a horror movie. I know I shouldn't, but I can't stop myself from looking. The blood looks black in the moonlight, but even without color, my lizard brain knows exactly what it is. My vision starts to gray out and I struggle to keep myself conscious. I reach up to rub my right temple to try and clear my head but pull my hand back when I touch wetness.

Did I fall in a puddle?

Bringing my hand into my line of sight, I notice it's covered in a wet sticky substance. *How big of a puddle did I land in?* I look down and around me and there's no sign of moisture anywhere around me. In fact, the ground is extremely dry and hard...

My confusion leaves me when I see a drop of dark liquid fall to the ground in front of my face. I bring my hand closer to my face and sniff.

I don't even have time to lay back down before my vision completely blacks out... *Head wounds bleed a lot, don't they?*

Before the darkness completely consumes me, I hear a rustling noise from above. Letting out a whimper, I hope whatever it is happens to be an herbivore.

22

SPENCER

"SPENCER!"

Avery's panicked yell sends me crashing through the undergrowth. Her voice came from the direction of the area we've nicknamed the Canyon because of the topography. It's not too deep, but the drops are dangerous. Three sides are steep enough to be troublesome, but we've had to put a few animals out of their misery over the time we've been around when they have fallen from the northern drop... the side that Avery is standing atop of.

I never would have thought that her tracking abilities would surpass mine, but apparently hunting with your uncles trumps scout camp. Either way, she found his trail in under ten minutes from the time she got out of her car.

As I reach the edge of the canyon, I slow down to make sure I don't cause the ledge to crumble away beneath our feet. This side gets more and more unstable every year, and I can already see where parts have fallen away since the last time I was out here. Avery's light is pointed down into the bowl of the canyon, but I can't see what she's seeing yet.

The look she gives me when she faces my approach has my blood freezing in my veins.

"No," I tell her. "Tell me he is not down there. Tell me it's just another clue. It's not him putting that look on your face."

"Spence," she says, swallowing hard. "I can't tell from up here if he's just hurt or if he is... is..."

"You and the guys know how to get down there safely. I don't. I need your help to get to him. *He* needs your help."

The memories of all of the deer carcasses I've had to drag from the base of this drop-off keep flashing in my brain. If he is dead, I don't want to see it. I can't have that image in my head.

On the other hand, if Lucky is hurt badly enough that Avery can't tell from up here, every second counts. The thought that my hesitancy could cost him his life makes me move. I grab my friend's hand and start pulling her to the path that will get us safely into the bowl of the canyon to reach him. I can hear Avery praying as I lead her to him. I'm not a religious man, but I send a quick one up myself.

Please let him be alive.

I hear the sound of someone crashing through the bushes on the eastern side and call out a warning.

"You're coming up on the canyon! Slow the fuck down!"

"Sorry, Sir," Jace and Shiloh call out in unison as they break through the tree line. I pause to watch as they come to a stop, Shiloh perched on the back of the bigger man. The last thing we need is more people falling into the Canyon. Their flashlight sweeps the edge of the trees, and I realize they can be of some help.

"If you are okay with seeing it," I call out to them. "Shine your light down below the northern drop to keep an eye on Lucky until I can get him out. It looks like he fell."

Shiloh surprises me by climbing down and shining his light into the bowl of the canyon, sweeping slowly to find the man below. Jace hunches in on himself and backs away from the edge to lean against a tree. The big man doesn't have Lucky's blood phobia, but he isn't good with seeing people hurt. Our teddy man is going to need a lot of cuddles tonight.

I watch the beam roaming the Canyon floor while I go back to pulling Avery along the nearly invisible trail. The beam from Shiloh's flashlight is finally stationary as I enter from the southern end.

Lucky's broken body is under the spotlight, and it is obvious why Avery couldn't tell if he was alive or not. He is completely covered in blood. My hesitation lasts barely a second before I race over to him. I cannot lose him, not when I just found him again. My knees crash to the ground on his right side and I cautiously lift his wrist to check for his pulse.

He lets out a groan with the small movement. It's the most amazing sound in the world to me, but I still feel for his pulse. It's weak, but I can feel it. He's alive.

"Should we move him?" I ask Avery without taking my eyes off Lucky. "I mean you're not supposed to move a spinal injury, right?"

She's the one with the full CPR and trauma response training. Since our original plan since middle school was she was to be the field reporter to my photojournalist, she went full in on everything. We were going to be our own dynamic duo, but then life happened.

"Didn't hurt my back or neck," the man on the ground mumbles and I feel like I can breathe again.

23

LUCKY

The first sign that I have regained consciousness is the light beyond my eyelids. I kind of wish it wasn't there because the feeling of an ice pick being jammed into my brain reminds me that I have a head injury. I've taken enough spills from my horse as a kid to know it will hurt even worse to move at this point, so I don't even try.

The second sign that I'm back in the land of the living is hearing the panicked voice of Spencer and a woman. It takes me a minute to recognize her voice as that of the field reporter from Channel Eight. If I was dreaming, this would be a nightmare having the only person I've ever crushed on with a woman in front of me. However, them wondering if it was safe to move me disavowed me of the notion of a nightmare. They are both apparently here to rescue me from my own stupidity.

I was dumb for running in the woods at night. I know better.

"Little one, are you hurt anywhere else?" Spencer's

voice is right next to me, and I feel his hands roaming over my body, checking for injuries. "Open your eyes, baby. Let me check for a concussion."

A concussion would definitely explain the jack-hammer that has started demolition in my head. Hell, it might be an entire construction crew at this point. Maybe my father-in-law put out a hit on me and...

"Lucas Holloway, open your eyes right now!" Spencer demands, and I have no choice but to comply. I don't want him angry with me.

The light from above makes the pain worse and I try to turn away from it. A firm grip on my chin forces my head back to the pain inducing light. The whimpers falling from my lips are completely involuntary at this point, but I won't close my eyes and disappoint Spencer. Even with so much fucking pain...

"Shhh, Lucky," he whispers softly. "You're doing so well, baby. You can rest now."

The hand on my chin goes from forceful to a caress, but I'm starting to feel the pain elsewhere in my body now. Why am I hurting so much? I only bumped my head...

It feels like fire is engulfing my left arm as someone lifts me off the ground. Oh, yeah. I hurt my arm. That's where I first noticed the blood. The... blood...

"You're okay, Lucky," Shiloh's voice comes from nearby. The relief is undeniable in his tone, but I also hear the fear. "Daddy Spencer will take good care of you."

Daddy Spencer? I know I am not the most knowledgeable out there, but I am fairly certain that Spencer isn't married to Shiloh's mother. And there is definitely not a biological component going on...

"Kitty, don't confuse him right now," Spencer's voice comes from the pillow I'm resting on. "You two, go ahead and get my car started. We're going to the emergency room to get him checked out by a doctor."

I start to shake my head, but it hurts too much. I can't afford a trip to the hospital. Sabrina would never pay for it, and her father would withhold my pay. That means no more pizza.

"I don't want to lose my pizza," I whine into the pillow.

The pillow laughs at me, shaking and making my head hurt even worse.

"Pillows don't laugh," I say as my fist makes contact with the cotton under my cheek. "My head hurts more."

The laughter stops abruptly, and I settle in to try and get back to sleep. Maybe I can get back to the dreams where I am free of Sabrina and her family... the dreams with the big house and crazy men, especially the one that makes my heart race in a good way. He's the only one who has ever done that.

A woman's voice keeps me from fully drifting off. I don't want to hear her voice right now. Granted, she is not Sabrina, which is an improvement. But I still don't want to be listening to the news right now.

"I think you need to get him to the hospital sooner rather than later, Spence. He's not making any sense."

The giggle I let out turns into a moan, but the lady made a silly rhyme. Maybe she can stay after all...

"Ave," a sexy voice says with a hint of fear. "I'm gonna need you to drive."

I don't like the sexy voice sounding afraid...

24

SPENCER

The drive to the hospital was probably the most terrifying twenty minutes of my life. Lucky was in and out of consciousness, and when he was awake, it was like he didn't have a grasp on reality. He kept mentioning Sabrina and his in-laws and not being able to pay. Then, when we got to the emergency room, he begged us not to take away his pillow.

The doctor wanted to admit him for observation and there wasn't a chance in hell I was going to object to that. So now I am sitting in the most uncomfortable chair ever created watching the fifth or sixth nurse visit of the night to wake him up and ask him basic questions. The scans they took when we first came in showed slight bleeding and swelling, but the doctor says that as long as his condition doesn't get worse overnight, we should be able to take him home in the morning.

"How is he doing?" Jay asks, poking his head into the

room. "Eli and Eric are with the others so they don't bombard you guys."

I take the interruption as an opportunity to stretch for a bit since I know I won't be able to sleep until I know for certain Lucky will be alright. I'm going on over thirty-six hours of nothing more than cat naps, but I've done worse during finals. Jay comes fully into the room and joins me over by the window as I place my forehead on the cool glass.

"Not sure he would even recognize any of the guys just yet," I mutter as soon as my friend is close enough to hear. "He thinks the house and all of us are a vivid dream and that he is still married to Sabrina."

Jay turns toward the bed before sighing. "Is it too much to hope that he remembers only the good stuff?"

I scoff and turn to face the room. "What good stuff? His ex-wife essentially blackmailed him into a marriage where she treated him as her own personal bank and when the money ran out she made it so he couldn't get a job or even go back home to his parents.

"From what I discovered over the last few days, Lucky hasn't had much *good* in his life."

A commotion in the hallway has both Jay and I heading that way. It's bad enough that Lucky needs to be poked and prodded every hour or so. He shouldn't have to worry about what little sleep he manages to get being interrupted by inconsiderate asshats in the hallway at four in the morning. I indicate to Jay to stay in the room while I go out to check. I have a feeling I know who is out there.

Once I step into the hall, I have a clear view of the nurse's station. My suspicions were correct. Sabrina Carlisle is at the desk, berating the night nurse. I turn back into the room and get a nod from Jay. He heard it as well. She is trying to claim she is his wife to get information... over my dead body.

I march over to the desk and see the nurse pulling information up on the computer.

"Unless you need to look up the number for security or the police, you had better stop what you are doing," I say before I even reach them. The nurse looks up at me in relief, but Sabrina's gaze holds surprise.

"Spencer Wright? What a pleasant surprise," she puts on the charm, like she has no clue about my interview earlier this evening. She takes steps to approach me, but I brush past her to go to the nurse.

"What information is this woman asking for, and why were you giving it to her?" I demand.

The nurse looks concerned by my questions but considering she just saw me ten minutes ago in the room, she knows why I am here. "Mrs. Holloway was asking about her husband's condition and for the room number. She is upset she was not contacted when he was first brought in since she is his emergency contact."

I scoff at the answer and turn to "Mrs. Holloway" as I respond to the nurse.

"Ms. Carlisle here," I say, enjoying the flinch she makes at my tone, "is no longer married to Mr. Holloway. They are divorced. She has no legal standing to request any information, and if you provide anything to her regarding Mr. Holloway, he will sue this hospital and yourself for violating his rights as a patient."

Sabrina bristles at my words but recovers enough to do something stupid. She steps up to me and puts her filthy hand on my chest. "Spencer, come on. The divorce was only last week. He forced me to accept it. I still care about him."

I rip her hand away, not caring about the performance she puts on by grabbing her wrist, acting like I hurt her.

"Try your act somewhere else, Sabrina," I tell her, moving between her and the door to Lucky's room. "Remember that you are the one who hired me to get proof so you could file for divorce. *You* are the one who used my photographs to create a false narrative against your husband. *You* are the one who arranged everything so that I couldn't testify to what I actually found out and rushed the hearing.

"I know about the money. I know about the fake pregnancy. I know about you and James and the others. I know about you taking everything from him, including his family, with your lies. You will *never* have access to him again."

After I finish, Sabrina looks enraged, but I don't give a flying fuck. She is not getting into that room to hurt him more. She is not going to get any information to use against him. I'm certain if she hears that he has a head wound, she will find a way to use that against him to refute what we've found out. She is so focused on what I have said that she doesn't notice the sound of the elevator doors opening.

I smile at the sight of hospital security exiting the lifts and heading to the nurse at the desk. Sabrina is talking, but I stopped listening. As long as she isn't pushing to get to the hall behind me, she can run her mouth all she wants. I've been recording everything from the time I stepped into the hall. Being a P.I. on an active case helps me get all kinds of expedited affidavits from the court, especially when that case is regarding someone who manipulated them.

"...he is still just a weakling. He will have to take me back."

As the security guard nods at the night nurse and turns to head toward us, I look down at Sabrina. I know I'm giving her an evil smirk, but I don't care. I take great pleasure in her expression as security interrupts her to tell her she needs to leave. She starts screaming and pushing at me in an attempt to get to the rooms, but the guard grabs her by the arm and starts to drag her away.

The commotion brings Jay to the doorway, so I decide to fuck with her some more before she's carted off.

"Go back to resting, sweetheart," I call back to him. "Make sure she doesn't wake our boy."

Let her think I'm in a relationship with Jay and that we have a child in there. It's safer for Lucky if she doesn't know where he is. I already have to figure out how she found out he is here. When the elevator doors close with her inside, I turn back to the room. Jay is smirking at me from his perch on the edge of the bed.

He tilts his head to the side and that is how I notice Lucky is awake on his own for the first time since we found him in the woods.

"Hey, Sleeping Beauty," I tell him with a smile. "How are you feeling?"

25

LUCKY

The screeching of a banshee wakes me from the weirdest dream I think I have ever had. It had a drag queen and a laughing pillow and a cute black cat and...

"The woman already took all of my money, does she need to take my sleep, too?" I grumble and try to turn onto my side. The pinching feeling on my arm and pain in my head make me wake up in a hurry.

I open my eyes and sit up, only to notice I am not at home. Based on the IV in my arm and the machines surrounding the bed I am currently in, I appear to be in the hospital. This isn't good. I can't afford to be in a hospital, especially in a private room. Sabrina will never give me the money for it, not without making me do something I will really regret.

A throat clearing brings my attention to the man at the foot of the bed. He looks vaguely familiar, but I can't place him. "I'm sorry, but do I know you?" I ask. "I think I hit my head and it's a bit fuzzy. Did my wife send you?"

The man startles a bit at my question, but he motions to the foot of the bed asking if he can sit. I start to nod but realize quickly it isn't a good idea. Instead, I lift my arm to indicate that it's alright with me if he perches there.

"Lucky, you had a fall earlier tonight. The docs say the bump on your head seems to have affected your short-term memory."

He called me Lucky, not Lucas, not Mr. Holloway. The only person who calls me Lucky is Gramps...

"Did Gramps send you?"

The guy looks sad at my question but shakes his head. "No, I don't know Gramps. Is that your grandfather?"

I start to nod again. The pain makes me wince and I lean back against the pillows. At least the guy is nice enough to help me raise the bed up to a full sitting position. Head wounds are apparently still a bitch. Although this is the first time one has landed me in the hospital for a stay. All of this is a new experience.

"So, Mr. Stranger, how much of my memory has been wiped out?" I ask when he sits back down. "I can only assume our meeting is one of those things that I don't remember."

"Technically, this is the first time we've met, but that's only because I work retail on the overnight shifts and drive rideshare on the nights I am not scheduled. I'm off for the week, but I had already left the house when they brought you home the other night," he tells me. "My name is Jay, and I gotta say you have some good taste in your anime, little dude."

I chuckle as he points to the sneakers under the chair in the corner, but even that causes enough pain to force a wince. Jay pats my foot and explains about how I showed up at the bar owned by his landlord the other day and his housemates brought me home like a stray animal.

I'm not sure how much of his story is true, but something inside of me tells me I should believe it. I mean, at least the drag queen in my dreams makes sense now.

A woman in the hall starts screaming at someone, and my entire body tenses at the sound. I know who that is unfortunately, and they won't be able to keep her out.

"Is it too late to go back and die instead of whatever happened to me?" I ask Jay, only half joking. "I really don't want to deal with my wife right now."

He looks at me strangely and says, "Ex-wife, you mean, right? You guys are divorced now."

"Really?" I can feel my soul getting lighter. There's no fighting the smile on my face at the thought. "Oh, please God let it be true."

I put my palms together and lift my head as much as I can without it hurting. Jay chuckles at the end of the bed before getting up to go to the door. Sabrina's screeching seems to be getting farther away when he comes back to sit. A moment later, another guy comes in the room.

This one seems even more familiar to me than Jay. While he's looking at Jay with a bit of a grumpy look on his face, I'm studying him. I remember him, not his name but his face. He helped me at the Theta party. Yeah, that night kind of screwed me in the long run, but this guy took it upon himself to help a stranger. Judging by the fact that he's here with me now, he did it again.

He's also been the main fixation of my fantasies for the last year and a half. The memory of his hands on me was the only thing that has ever made me think I might be more than asexual. I still don't feel like I want sex, but touching and intimacy? This is the only person who has ever made me want those on more than a platonic or familial level.

"Hey, Sleeping Beauty," he says when he turns to me. At least he's stopped scowling. "How are you feeling?"

"Like I fell off a cliff," I tell him, not really knowing why I say those words. I meant to say "like shit" but I don't want to swear around this guy for some reason.

The guy lights up at my answer, but that is extinguished as soon as Jay speaks up.

"He doesn't remember, Spence. He didn't even know he was divorced. We're dealing with at least two weeks of memory loss."

"Is that your name? Spence?" I ask, trying to get him to be happy again. I liked seeing him happy. The smile he sends my way isn't the exuberant one from a second ago, but it's better than the scowl.

"Spencer Wright," he tells me, grabbing my left hand and placing a kiss to the back of my knuckles. "Private investigator and the man who was hoping to get to know you better before you took your little tumble in the woods."

My breath comes a little faster in response to his words, but I'm not scared. I think I might be excited. I haven't felt *that* in … well, ever. This is even better than my memories.

26

LUCKY

After spending the whole day Saturday and subsequent
night in the hospital, Spencer and Jay brought me back to
the manor house they share with six other guys. I guess
everyone was at work or church or something when we
got there because no one was around as they helped me
up to the room on the top floor. No one has given me
specifics, but I guess I moved in here the other day before
my fall.

Apparently, I met some of the guys at the bar at the
bottom of the hill when my car broke down the other
night. My best guess is they told me the room was open
for rent and I begged for it. Considering all of my stuff is
in the room already, it only makes sense. Even though I
don't know exactly what led up to my tumble in the
woods, I know that these guys did me a huge favor by
putting me up.

I'm not surprised that Sabrina figured out a way to
get a quick divorce and frame me for the one thing that

would get her money. What is catching me off guard is the lengths she went to, according to what Jay told me on the drive over. I knew the woman was devious, but I didn't think she was downright evil.

"You gonna be alright if I go out to work on a case?" Spencer pokes his head into my room while I am busy pulling items out of the boxes full of things that I don't even remember packing. "Jay won't hear if you need anything, but Eli just got home. He's in the room beneath yours, so if it hurts to yell you can just drop a book or something and he'll come up."

Despite the headaches I still get, I have to laugh in response. The way that he's acting is just so overprotective.

"Yes, Daddy," I say in response to his overprotective nature. Hopefully he can take a joke because I don't think I can take my attention away from the jewelry box I just unburied.

I thought I had lost this, but I am glad that I didn't. My grandfather's pocket watch and great-grandparents' rings should be in there. He gave those to me on my wedding day and told me that he hopes I will hand those down to my kid. Of course, the kid never happened, but I never got the chance to give them back to him.

He didn't use the rings for his own wedding since his parents were still alive when he got married. It should have been my mother to use them, but of course the tiny stones were too tacky for her. I would have loved to use them for my own wedding, but those rings should used when the couple is in love.

As for the watch. I used to pull that out of Gramp's nightstand all of the time when I was little. Gramps always said that Grandma Juliet was his one and only true love. He told me the stories about Grandma and how she was a "cheeky little ray of sunshine" around the house. She was with him before he got rich. She loved to make him laugh, even when she didn't remember who he was. I never had the chance to meet her, since she passed from Alzheimer's complications about five years before I was born.

She gave him that watch when they opened the riding school. Gramps gave me the most precious items he has, and they should be in this box. Pulling the jewelry box into my lap, I sit on the bed and debate if I should open it and check.

The hand on my shoulder makes me jump, but hearing Spencer's voice helps me to settle almost immediately.

"I know you didn't mean to say it, Little One, but please don't call me that unless you understand the meaning behind it."

I glance up at him in confusion, but I have to save the questions for another time. Right now, I need to find the courage to open this box and see if the bitch stole the most precious items I have ever been given.

"Lucky?" Spencer is crouching in front of me, hands on top of mine holding the box. "Are you alright? Did you hear me?"

I lift my gaze from the box in my hands to his face. The look of concern he is giving me makes me upset. I don't want him to be upset. He's done nothing but be nice to me and help me. I don't want to burden him any more than I already have, but...

"I'm scared," I whisper.

I feel his hands grip a little bit tighter before he gently takes the box from me and sets it on the bed beside me. Taking my hands in his, he asks, "Of me?"

There is no question about that, so I shake my head fast enough to make me dizzy. When I lift my right hand up to grip the side of my head, Spencer stands and pulls me up enough to take my seat on the bed. Before I can complain, he maneuvers me onto his lap, wrapping his arms around me. The dizziness is slowly going away as I listen to his heartbeat. I have a vague memory of a pillow laughing before he is talking to me again.

"Why are you scared, Little One?"

I shrug and reach for the box, pulling it into my lap. "It's dumb," I tell him, but he just taps me on the nose. That makes me smile, but just a little bit. I'm still too scared for a big smile.

"I know what *should* be in this box, but I'm scared that she might have taken them out."

Spencer squeezes me in a quick hug before putting his hand on top of the box.

"Will it bother you more to find out they are missing or not knowing if Sabrina has something so important to you?" he asks me.

"Either is bad," I shrug. "But if that bitch took my Gramp's watch, I'll kill her."

The chuckle from the man holding me makes me

realize I said that out loud. I guess I have my answer. I purse my lips together tightly to prevent any other unseemly outbursts from escaping. Mother would have a field day with my language today.

"Do you want me to open it?" he asks me, and I nod slowly. I don't want the dizzies to come back. I might be brave enough to look, but not if I have to be the one to open it. When his hand starts to lift the lid, I can't help it. I cover my eyes with my hands. If I don't see them missing, I don't have to make a decision about going back.

I feel Spencer's hands pulling my arms away from my face, so I squeeze my eyes shut. I'm not ready to look. He can't make me.

27

SPENCER

A part of me feels guilty for just bringing Lucky home without him knowing that he never actually agreed to stay here. Some of the guilt went away when I saw that the guys had already moved his stuff up to the room across from mine on the top floor while we were gone. Not having to argue with him about staying was a definite bright spot to the day I did not expect.

My phone alerts me to an email while I'm secretly watching the man unpack. Since he hasn't shown any of the warning signs the doctor told us to look out for, I take the opportunity to check what the email is since it is the business email, not my personal one.

From: amsavage@familydivision.ac.pa.gov

To: spencer@mr_wright_investigations.com

Subject: Regarding Carlisle v. Holloway

A LITTLE DISCOVERY

Greetings, Mr. Wright,

It has come to our attention that you never received the summons for the hearing of Carlisle v. Holloway in family court at the end of the previous month. Judge Roberts was greatly distressed at the revelations you made to the media before addressing them with the court. He would like to request a meeting to get further information on your findings in the investigation you were hired to conduct for Ms. Carlisle.

Please respond to this email or call to schedule an appointment. Judge Roberts has cleared his schedule for today to accommodate as this is time sensitive to his findings.

Looking forward to your response,
Alexandria Savage
Personal Assistant to Judge Michael Roberts

Well, this is happening faster than anticipated. I expected them to at least wait until Monday morning to contact me about Avery's exclusive from Friday night. Pulling my door closed, I put the phone number from the email though the reverse number search that I have for my P.I. business. I wouldn't put it past Sabrina to try and trick me with something like this, but the number is legit. A little bit of digging and I confirm that Alex Savage is indeed the assistant to the judge who made the ruling on Lucky's divorce. Having verified all of the information, I call the number.

"Alex Savage," the voice on the other end answers. "Either you are Spencer Wright, or you have a death wish for interrupting my mimosa time. Which one is it?"

"Spencer Wright at your service," I respond with a laugh. "I was not expecting to hear from anyone until tomorrow morning at the earliest. What time is the judge free? I have time, but I have to arrange for someone to be home with..."

I blank on what to refer to Lucky as. To me, he's already mine. But he doesn't know that yet, with or without the memory loss. I guess to others he would be a housemate? For now, at least that would be the best descriptor, but she doesn't give me a chance to label it.

"I am aware that Mr. Holloway is staying at your residence, Mr. Wright," Alex says into the silence. "The judge and I are also aware of the altercation at the hospital. I am a damn thorough assistant and *that* is the reason he's paying me out the ass to handle this on a weekend."

Her brusque nature is refreshing.

"One of my housemates should be home shortly," I say. "I can head out as soon as I know he's here. I don't want Mr. Holloway home alone, just in case."

Alex gives me an address and says that Judge Roberts is scheduled to be there for the next two hours. If I can't make it in that time frame, I'm supposed to text her so that she can find out where he is going to be. He is willing to work around my schedule. But he wants to have everything in order before the courts open on Monday morning.

I pop my head into Lucky's room to tell him I have to

step out, and his response has all the neurons in my body firing at once. I've never had that strong of a reaction to a guy calling me "Daddy" like I just had with Lucky. I've scened with other boys, even tried dating a few, but nothing has ever felt as *right* as hearing that word falling from Lucky's lips.

Seeing how distracted he is by his packing, I don't think he is even aware of what he said, so I give him a gentle warning. Based on the lack of response, I'm pretty sure he isn't even paying attention to me at this point.

When I try and get his focus on me, he spooks badly. When I ask if he's scared of me, he assures me in the most adorable way that he's not. Somehow, this man has started to fall into little headspace without ever having realized he is a little. Pulling him into my lap is both the greatest feeling ever, and one of the hardest things I've had to deal with. There's a level of guilt sitting in my gut from him not having all of his memories. He was so mad at me when he ran off into the woods. Until he remembers that and why he was angry, I can't let myself fully enjoy this.

When I open the lid of the box for him, he is just too cute covering his eyes. I gently pull his hands away from his face, only to discover his eyes squeezed shut, his face scrunched up like he's sucking on a lemon. He is perfect in every way, and I just want to cuddle him forever.

"You have to look, Lucky-boy," I lean down and whisper in his ear. "Only you will know if something is missing."

He slowly opens one eye, and whatever he sees in the

box makes him open both and reach out for the contents of the jewelry box in a hurry. I have to tighten my hold on him to make sure he doesn't fall, like the jewelry box does after he grabs whatever he needs from it. The items he grabs out don't appear to be much, but by the way he's clutching them to his chest, they are priceless to him.

28

SPENCER

The address Alex gave me to meet the judge corresponds to a massive estate with a box that I can only assume is an intercom at the gate. When I pull up, I have no idea what to do. I wasn't given any further instructions. There is not a button to press or anything. I don't even see a place for a card or a code...

"State your name and purpose," comes a voice from the speaker. They probably think I'm lost. Lord knows my seven year old Toyota is not the type of vehicle they are used to seeing.

"Uh," I stutter for a moment before clearing my throat to start again. "My name is Spencer Wright and I'm here to see Judge Roberts."

There is no response for what seems like forever, but the gate starts to open. Before I pull forward, the voice on the intercom gives me directions of where to park and where to go. Apparently, the judge is in the stables. Being a city boy from a solidly middle-class family, I am thoroughly lacking knowledge on which outbuilding is which, but luckily there are signs pointing the way.

When I round the corner in the path leading to the stables, according to the signs, I can see two older gentlemen having a conversation outside of the building. I slow my approach so as not to interrupt them, but one of the men waves me over as soon as he notices me.

"Mr. Wright, I presume?" he asks and looks delighted at my affirmation. Pointing to himself he introduces himself. "I am Judge Michael Roberts and this is Mr. Joseph Grable, Mr. Holloway's grandfather. He is *also* very interested in what you have found out about Ms. Carlisle's accusations and actions over the past year."

I'm in the process of shaking the man's hand when his name registers.

"Any relation to Eli Grable?" I ask and he jerks like he just got zapped by static electricity. His heavy gaze searches my face for something. Whatever it is, he apparently gets his answer then nods.

"Eli Hawthorne, you mean," he says. "How do you know my son?"

"He's one of my roommates, Sir," I tell him and step back so that the judge isn't excluded and we can get back on track. "I think I'm gonna have to have a conversation with him when I get back to the house about secrets, though. He never said anything about being related to Lucky, or one of the richest men on this continent for that matter."

At that, the old man lets out a hearty laugh. "No, I'm sure he didn't. Never cared about the money, that one. As for how he relates to my grandson, Elliot has been over-protective of Lucky his entire life, outside of the month or so he was jealous after me and his mama split up. He even wanted to give up his own inheritance to the boy when he found out the other night what that sorry excuse for a woman did to him. I had to tell the lawyers not to answer his calls until Monday."

Here I was thinking that Eli was growing soft. I mean, yeah, he *can* comfort a sub in distress, but he will usually pawn the job off to a care giver type if possible. It usually takes him weeks, if not months, to open up to a new sub in the house. He has been taking the initiative and running interference for Lucky from the minute he saw him. It was out of character, so I was worried I had competition for my boy's affections... Damn sadist...

"And here I was thinking it was just going to be another Sunday morning riding lesson for my grandson," Judge Roberts says, clapping each of us on a shoulder. "Let's take this discussion somewhere more private while the kiddo is distracted."

Joe shrugs and leads the way toward what appears to be a small house. "We can use Jessie's office while she's giving Oscar his lesson."

When we're all seated in the office, Joe directs my attention to the wall of photographs behind him, specifically the ones showing a happy and smiling Lucky sitting up on the back of a horse as a child.

"Lucky was always the brightest sun here at the ranch," he tells us. "That is, until his mother figured out that Jessie, my right-hand gal around here, is also a daughter of mine. Her mother was a night of grief sex after my father passed, which Nadine never forgave me for. I went through about a decade or so, sleeping around and heavy drinking. My Juliet got me the help I needed for my addictions, but Nadine never forgave me for fathering other kids and watering down her inheritance. Her mother kept her mostly in line, though, so the young ones were safe enough from her venom as they grew up.

"Unfortunately, Lucky suffered the worst for it. He was about twelve or thirteen when it was found out that I had one of my daughters working here around her perfect *legitimate* son, and Nadine stopped bringing him out here. It was years before he set foot here again.

"Once he started college, he came back as often as he could without his mother finding out, but then that other one got her claws in him...

"I haven't spoken to or seen my only grandson in over a year, not since that joke of a wedding reception. I know you just met him, but please tell me they didn't take his smile."

There is anguish in the old man's voice, and his friend pats his arm in a comforting gesture. His eyes are pleading with me to give him good news, but I don't know what to tell him. The only time I've seen Lucky really smile was the flash of relief at finding the watch and rings in that box.

"He hasn't really had much to smile about since I've met him, Sir," I tell him, trying to hedge as much as possible. "But he's not broken. Not yet at least. I think he got away from her in time, though, based on what I managed to dig up over the past couple of days."

"And that brings us to why we are here, sweating our balls off in this tiny office," Judge Roberts cuts in. "You both alright with me recording this? Need it all legal and up and up for the judge taking over the criminal side of things."

We nod as the man sets an old-fashioned pocket recorder, complete with miniature cassette, on the desk. At my look of surprise, he chuckles.

"It's less likely to be accused of tampering in this form. Digital manipulation is a lot easier than splicing a cassette tape," he explains before he presses the record button. "Today is August the twenty-second and the time is one twenty-seven in the afternoon. I, Judge Michael Roberts, am here with private investigator of record Spencer Wright to get his testimony regarding his investigations into Mr. Lucas Anthony Holloway on behalf of Ms. Sabrina Carlisle and the subsequent investigation into Ms. Carlisle herself.

"Mr. Wright, do I have permission to record you for the duration of this conversation, understanding you have the right to revoke that consent at any time?"

"Yes," I say. "I understand and give my consent to have this conversation recorded."

The judge nods and turns back to the recorder. "Also present is Mr. Joseph Grable, grandfather of Mr. Holloway, as witness to the conversation held here today. Mr. Grable, do I have your consent to record you for the duration with the understanding you have the right to revoke your consent at any time?"

"Yes, Michael," he says. "Now let's get this all on record already."

The judge chuckles before asking me to start from the beginning. I don't want to be here all day, but I also refuse to leave anything out.

"Sabrina Carlisle sent me multiple emails requesting me to investigate her husband, Mr. Holloway, starting in April. By the second Friday in May, she was sending multiple requests per day. I never even wanted to take the case, but I was accepted into a study abroad program for my photography. My scholarship only covered half of the costs, and I had three days to come up with the rest of the money to secure my spot.

"I'll admit that I over-charged Ms. Carlisle compared to my usual fee. I adjusted it up so that the deposit would cover the funds I needed. I told myself that if she was willing to pay a five-thousand-dollar deposit, it would mean she was certain of his infidelity, and I would not have to deal with her beyond handing over a few photographs.

"The investigation resulted in zero proof of infidelity, at least on the part of Mr. Holloway..."

I spend the next hour relaying all of the information I discovered, as well as what I put in my report that was supposed to be filed into evidence. I even share everything I have learned since getting home about how Sabrina and her lawyers falsified my address and that someone didn't follow procedures for my summons through the court system itself.

"Who the hell was responsible for that, Mike?" Joe speaks up while I take a swig of water. "You mean to tell me my grandson lost everything because someone in your office is either incompetent or dirty?"

Judge Roberts shakes his head before answering verbally, "I can assure you, the person responsible for the summons *will* be questioned and investigated in this matter. Anything else to add to it, son?"

At the looks from the men, I figure we have been at this for a while.

"Just that she showed up in the early hours Saturday morning at the hospital after Mr. Holloway was admitted following an accident," the panicked look on Joe's face makes me rush to continue. "He suffered a minor concussion with some trauma related memory loss, but he's otherwise fine. He just doesn't remember the last couple weeks.

"Anyways, she showed up at the hospital while myself and another of the guys from the house were sitting with Lucky, er, Mr. Holloway. She told the night nurse that she was his wife and demanded to know where he was and what his condition was. When the nurse hesitated, she demanded information and threatened legal action because, and I quote, you can't keep a wife from knowing her husband's condition.

"I know I don't have to tell you this, Judge, but she was pushing that nurse to break the law to get that information. I am still looking into how she knew he was even there. We didn't call anyone, and we filled out the intake forms as Lucky Hollow, not Lucas Holloway. He was so worried about Ms. Carlisle chastising him for wasting money on a hospital trip that we thought it better to tie everything up with a small lie until he wasn't talking about laughing pillows and pizza thieves.

"Before she could get anything from the nurse, I interrupted, and she was escorted away by security after a verbal altercation with myself. I will admit to you now, I recorded everything she said to me when I confronted her. It was in accordance with the regulations that protect me in the active investigation of a case, but I have not yet reviewed the conversation in depth.

"I was more concerned with keeping her away from Mr. Holloway in his vulnerable state than paying attention to what she was saying."

The two men in front of me nod and make noises of agreement.

"I'll want a copy of that recording, Mr. Wright," the judge says. "It won't be logged in as evidence for this case, but I want to include your case findings in my petition to the district attorney to file charges against Ms. Carlisle. At this time, I believe this concludes our conversation, are we agreed?"

Both Joe and I give our statements agreeing and Judge Roberts turns off the recorder.

"Off the record," he says standing up and putting the recorder back into his pocket. "Your son isn't the only Sadist in town, Joe. Your grandson is going to get everything back and then some after I'm through with the whole lot of them. No one gets to use me like that and get away with it."

As we walk back toward the parking lot, I see Joe pull out his phone when he turns in the direction of the main house.

"Elliot! Why is this the first I'm hearing about Lucky being in the hospital?," I hear him say before he disappears inside.

I really need to have a talk with our resident Sadist about what is and isn't acceptable to keep hidden.

29

LUCKY

The first thing I see when I wake up from my nap is my grandfather's watch on the pillow next to me. *The bitch didn't take it.* The relief of it being in the box was enough to exhaust me earlier. I don't even remember what else was in the jewelry box aside from this watch and the rings, but I have what matters. The crash from the adrenaline was so severe, I could barely keep my eyes open. The doctor *had* mentioned that I would need to sleep more often, but I didn't think the drowsiness would hit me like this. Having Spencer tuck me in was a unique experience.

I vaguely recall a kiss to my forehead, but I was halfway asleep already. Some people might feel strange being treated like a child, but I kind of enjoyed it. Letting Spencer take the lead like that was a revelation for me. Growing up, I was always calmer when I had someone to tell me what is expected of me, what the next steps are. The anxiety of making decisions paralyzes me, especially if I know my decisions will affect someone other than just myself.

It's not even the decisions that bother me. It is what happens after. My parents have always drilled it into me that I have to be viewed a certain way, not bring shame or disgrace to the Holloway name. If I make a wrong decision, it can be disastrous and cost a lot of money and effort to fix it. I've seen it enough with my father's family to the point that I prefer to leave the decisions to someone else. At least then, I don't have to deal with guilt on top of the anxiety.

In my experience, people make decisions on my behalf based on society's views or their own personal gain. My mother does it. My wife does it... EX...ex-wife. *I must remember that.* I hate how their choices make me feel, yet it is all I've ever known. Letting them make all of the decisions means I'm less likely to be noticed. Being invisible has saved my booty many times over the years. I had almost succeeded in having everyone forget that Lucas Anthony Holloway even exists.

How Spencer treated me earlier, and even yesterday in the hospital, was completely different from what my family has done in the past. He made some decisions for me, but the reason always seemed to be for my benefit or well-being. If he has a selfish reason for what he's done for me, I can't see it. I want more of that in my life. Now that I've had a taste, I'm craving it.

Maybe whatever brought me to him is a good thing, even if I can't remember what it was. Between the party and whatever happened this time, it feels like the stars are aligning to pull us together. Setting down the watch next to the rings on the nightstand, I chuckle at my silliness. Fate doesn't exist.

Climbing out of bed, I notice someone talking outside my room, and it makes me curious. I'm usually not one to snoop around, but something is telling me that it will be fun to play spy. I haven't been able to do this since I was a little kid at Gramps's house. Cracking open the door, I drop quietly into a crouch to sneak into the common area on this floor. Spencer's door is closed, so I can only assume he is still out on his case.

"...haven't told anyone yet, Dad."

I find the source of the voice once I peek around the edge of the sofa. There is a guy leaning against the countertop, next to the fridge, in the small kitchen area, talking on his phone. He is only a couple of inches taller than I am, if that, but muscular enough to not be a lazy sack of bones like me.

"Yes, Dad," he says turning to open the fridge. "I will make sure he eats... I know, Dad... I won't... Oh, come on!"

He stands up and slams the door after grabbing a can of pop and winces at the sound. Glancing toward the rooms, he cocks his head before saying, "I think he's up now. Gotta go. Love ya. Bye."

I dive behind the sofa, pulling my arms over my head. If I can't see him, he can't see me, right?

"Where oh where could Lucky have run off to?" he asks in a sing song voice. "I swear he must be magic to disappear into thin air like that."

He can't see me!

I can't stop the giggle that escapes, and I pop both hands over my mouth to try and hold it in.

"Huh? I thought I heard a fairy laugh," the man says as his footsteps head toward the stairs that go down into the rest of the house.

I count to twenty Mississippis before I get my feet back under me to get up. I peek over the top of the sofa and don't see anyone, so this time I let the giggle fly free. The silly man didn't even look hard for me. Hiding is thirsty work, so I tiptoe toward the fridge for a drink. I hope there's juice. Pop tickles my nose and feels funny.

"So that's where you were hiding," the man says from right behind me.

I scream as all my limbs go flailing. I would have hit the floor had the man not grabbed me. Gravity tends to not like me lately, judging by the still there bump on my head.

"Lucky, I'm so sorry," he says. "Are you alright? I was just messing around."

I nod, gulping in air and trying to keep my heart inside of my chest. My head seems to be pounding in time with my heart, and my stomach seems to want to come to the outside of my body. My feet are under me, but they don't seem to have gotten the memo that they are supposed to be holding me up, so I'm really happy that this man is strong enough to keep me upright. I mean, I am barely one hundred thirty pounds, but I'm still a grown man.

Footsteps pound up the stairs and a for really reals

giant is in front of me. It takes me a second to recognize the look on his face is one of concern, not anger. Right behind him are two other guys who are normal sized, one of which has a line of cobalt blue eyeliner going to his hairline.

"O.M.G. Lucky," the one in makeup says when he realizes there's no emergency. "Give a girl a heart attack why doncha?"

The man holding me up is shaking. Before I can even start to worry that I'm too heavy for him, he breaks into laughter with the others chuckling along. I'm glad it was laughter and not my weight because my legs are still rubber.

"Eric?" the giant says and the man in question looks at him softly. "I think you should go check the mirror."

We all watch as the makeup wearing man, who I now know is Eric, sashays into the tiny bathroom muttering about horror movies and running up stairs. There's an anticipatory silence until he flips on the light, and then everyone else erupts in laughter when he lets out a string of profanity that would make a sailor blush before stomping back down the stairs.

Finally feeling strong enough to not fall over, I push away from my tormentor-slash-savior to sit on the sofa. He takes the seat next to me while the giant and remaining normal sized guy lean against the counter. I have to admit, for someone super introverted like me, no one here is setting off any alarm bells. My whole existence, except when I get to be on the back of a horse, is nothing but tension and anxiety. It doesn't make any sense for me to feel at ease, but I am going to roll with it.

The guy next to me, phone call guy, turns to me and puts a hand on my knee. "Lucky," he pulls my attention to his face with the tone of his voice. It's not angry, but there's a force to it that means he expects me to listen to him. "Has any of your memory come back yet?"

I shake my head slowly to avoid the headache coming back, but I don't lose the smile on my face. "From what I've pieced together, whatever happened to cause me to end up here was bad enough," I tell him. "I don't know if I want to remember."

Phone guy sighs and looks at the other two before he pulls his hand away. I kind of miss the contact. I'd never gotten the opportunity to be a tactile person since I was a little kid. Sabrina only touches me in front of my parents, but her touch gives me the yucks. No one else ever bothered except for Gramps before Mother cut me off from him. I think at one point there were cousins or maybe the staff kids, but I was so young that I can't remember if they were real of just imaginary friends.

"I guess we can do introductions again," the man next to me says. "Or rather, for the first time since I don't think we *actually* introduced ourselves properly earlier.

"The big guy over there is Jace," he says while the giant gives me a shy smile and wave. "He looks like a big bad biker gang leader, but he is our resident teddy bear, sometimes referred to as T.B. for short. If you ever need a hug for any reason, or no reason at all, he's your go to."

The other guy leaning against the counter stands up

straight and waves next. He has the proper posture of someone who has either been in the military or had to take etiquette lessons, like I did. He looks too young for having served, so I can only assume he got really used to balancing books on his head growing up.

"My name is Scott," he says, relaxing back after shaking out the stiff posture. "Resident switch and house chef. Let me know if there are any foods you can't have..."

He pauses for a second considers his words before he continues "I mean like allergy or intolerance wise, not something someone told you that you aren't allowed to eat. If your Daddy says you can't have something that you want, just let me know. I'm good at secret snack parties."

Jace starts nodding emphatically next to Scott, but I am confused. Why would my father have any say in what I eat when I'm living here? He didn't even care when I lived under his roof. So why would he care now? My brain must be more scrambled from the fall than I thought.

"Why does my father have a say in my food?"

The two men in front of me look at me like I've said the sky is made of tapioca pudding, but phone guy grabs my knee again before saying, "Scott said your *Daddy*, not your father, Lucky. Those are two completely different things."

Turning to the other two, he tilts his head toward the stairs and says, "Guys, why don't you head down to the main kitchen and bake us up some cookies while I try to fill Lucky in on some things that we might have over-looked pointing out before moving him in."

The two of them nod in unison before stomping down the stairs. I hear the door close below which lets me know that me and the phone guy are alone on the top floor. With it being just the two of us now, I grab one of the throw pillows and hug it to my chest and turn to give him my full attention.

"Alrighty then," I wiggle around a bit to make sure I'm as comfy as I'm going to get. "What did I miss in the introductory course? I can promise, I am an excellent student."

30

LUCKY

The guy in front of me chuckles before mirroring my pose, sans pillow, leaning against the other armrest of the sofa to face me. I have a niggling feeling like I should know him... beyond whatever memories I lost from the last week or so. There is something extremely familiar about this guy.

"So what I'm gonna tell you here is something that no one else in the house even knows," he says as he leans in toward me. "You are the first one under this roof to know this, okay?"

I bounce in my excitement. I love being the first to know about something. I can't *keep* a secret to save my life, but I love hearing them. Nodding emphatically, I wave my hands at him to continue.

"Firstly, since you don't remember it, my name is Eli."

I give him a slow nod to acknowledge what he's said, but that can't be the secret. He's purposefully drawing this out, but that's alright. It's like a game. Games are fun. I miss games.

"My name is Elliot Hawthorne, but that wasn't the name I was born with. My full name from before my step-father legally adopted me was Elliot Joseph Grable. I believe you know my birth father?"

How would I...

NO WAY!

"You're one of Gramps's bastards?!"

I wince as soon as the words are out of my mouth. That woman's poison has no business coming from my lips.

"I'm so sorry," I hurry and stammer out. "That d-didn't come out right. It's just that my mother... My mother said... for my entire life..."

Eli reaches over and grips my knee to get me to stop with the word vomit apologies. Looking up into his face, he's smiling. Either he's got a thing about not liking people in pain, or he really is as nice as he seems.

"I know what your mother thinks of me, Lucky," he says. "She never did get the point of the whole big sister thing. Her harassment is the reason Mom left Dad and I wasn't able to play with you anymore. I was seven and you were about four at the time. She made Dad choose between having me in his life or having you."

So I really did have other kids to play with once upon a time? The relief I feel, knowing that not everything good in my childhood memories was wishful thinking, almost drowns out his next words.

"I was mad at you for a while since you got to spend

time with my dad when I couldn't," he says, making me sad. I was four. How could I be to blame?

"But Mom broke it down for me. I still had my mom to love me, even though I couldn't have my dad. Your grandfather was the only one left to show you love, so it wasn't fair to take that away from you."

I turn to face the kitchen again. I know I am dealing with a brain injury, but do these things really happen outside of soap operas? It is crazy enough finding out I have an uncle only three years older than I am, but somehow, I just randomly came to be living in his house. This can't be real. I feel like I must have forgotten something more to the story. He doesn't seem like he's finished talking to me.

Eli slides closer on the sofa and pulls me to his side. I don't fight it. I'm still in shock.

"I am not telling you this to make you feel guilty, Lucky," he says, kissing the top of my head when I let out a sniffle.

When did I start crying?

"Dad, your grandfather, didn't want you to know our connection for this very reason. He said you grew up to take on everyone else's burden but won't lay your own down. You barely even admit they exist," Eli says as he gives me a squeeze.

"But, you aren't alone anymore, Lucky. You have your Uncle Eli to help you carry them. You also have every person in this house, and a few outside of it, whether you want them or not. When you put together a couple Daddies, a Sadist, a switch, a teddy bear, a puppy, a kitten, and a bratty drag queen you can accomplish anything."

I hiccup a giggle before I pull back to look up into his face. "What do you mean by Daddies? You said before that you didn't mean my father, but I don't get it."

My new-found Uncle Eli spends the next hour or so giving me a full run-down of age play and what a Daddy can be to a little or middle or even a submissive partner, referred to as a boy or girl. A Daddy basically gets his purpose and pleasure from helping his partner in ways that allow them to give up control. Sometimes it involves taking over completely, while other times it is just in the bedroom. Sometimes, there is no sexual component to it at all.

"Do you mean like a sugar daddy?" I ask, trying to wrap my head around what he is saying.

"Sugar Daddies are part of it," Eli explains. "There are many different ways a man can be a Daddy, but for your sake, I am only going to focus on the ones in the house. When you recover fully from the fall, we can go deeper into it all."

Eli points out how he believes I am a little, which I can't refute once he is done giving me examples. That floaty, carefree place I went to when Spencer was taking care of me earlier is something I want to experience more of, only on purpose next time. The fun and games side of me that has been peeking out really makes me want to explore a lot more. When he mentions sippy cups and swirly straws I can't hide my excitement.

"We are going to have to get you a stuffie," he says

when I keep reacting to everything he mentions. "I don't think we can afford to lose pillows from this couch. It's ancient and needs as much padding as it can get."

I giggle at the thought of hoarding all of the pillows until Eli starts a brief rundown of how everyone else in the house fits into things. He explains that he is technically a Sadist and a Dom, but he is very particular about who he plays with and when. Most of the people in the house and at the bar haven't seen him in a scene yet. Then, in response to my confusion, he explains what a scene is and how it affects dynamics within relationships and play with others.

When I say I think I understand what he means, he continues in the house introductions. I really don't understand most of it, but that is what the internet is for. Research is fun for me, and I retain information better in visual format.

He tells me Spencer is a Daddy looking for a little. Eli doesn't go into too much detail, claiming that Spencer will want to explain it himself. That works for me. My being a little and the man I like being a Daddy looking for one seems like kismet, if I believed in that bippity boppity stuff.

"Jay is a Daddy, like Spencer, but more into the *funishments* and looking for a brat. He wants someone who is going to push his buttons," he says, breaking into my thoughts. The concept of purposely going against the rules makes me shiver. I guess it's a good thing I don't like Jay in that way.

Jace, the giant man, is a boy according to Eli. He is

submissive but doesn't do any kind of regression. I can totally see it from the little bit of interaction we had up here earlier. Eli tells me that it's been hard on Jace to find a Daddy or Mommy because they take one look at him and assume he's a Dom. I wrinkle my nose at that.

I want to find a way to help him find a Daddy. But he can't have Spencer. He is gonna be MY Daddy.

"Scott is a switch and a Middle, meaning he regresses to older adolescence. Sometimes he is the Dominant partner, needing to be in control, but when his Middle is active, he is submissive." Eli continues with his descriptions of everyone unaware that I'm having trouble focusing on anything beyond the man I want to be my very own Daddy.

"Toby and Shiloh, who you haven't met... yet... again?" He shakes his head. "Anyway, they are into pet play, as a puppy and kitten respectively. They basically roleplay as their animals, but it's more than that. They get into a headspace like you do when you regress to your little self, only they react like their animals would, not like a child."

It's all very confusing to me, but I can understand why people want to escape real life. I have been trying to get away from reality as far back as I can remember.

"And that, dear nephew, is the introduction to Kink Manor," Eli says before launching a tickle attack.

"YOU FORGOT ABOUT ME!" Eric's angry voice comes up from the bottom of the stairs.

Eli sits back up while I wipe the happy tears from my eyes. "And Eric, resident drama queen who has his nose in everybody else's business when he isn't up on stage as Miss Sassy Frass, the drag queen."

The man in question stomps into the room from the stairs, makeup corrected and fully transformative, and plops himself onto the sofa between us.

"Now what's this about a nephew?"

31

SPENCER

Pulling up at the house after my visit with the judge and Mr. Grable, it looks like we have a packed house based on the cars parked along the drive. Inside the foyer, there are definitely more shoes than just for those of us living here. I'm pretty sure I recognize Avery's favorite boots and Ash's signature Skechers among the pairs lined up neatly to the side of the rack. The smile on my face is genuine as I put my bargain bin knock off shoes in my cubbie. It looks like Sunday night movies are on for the first time in a while. The lingering smell of popcorn as I open the door from the entryway confirms it.

The fact that there is no one to be found on the first two floors of the house isn't surprising, considering our movie room is in the basement. Long before I moved in, someone had transformed the main room of the basement into a miniature theater, complete with projector. They even painted the walls dark shades of blue and purple and installed a kick-ass surround sound system.

Unfortunately, they didn't bother with proper seating before they moved out. We've been getting by with a few odds and ends thrown together, but some day it would be nice to finish fixing it up.

I race up the stairs to change out of my jeans and button-down shirt that smells suspiciously like horses, even though I was nowhere near the animals. Crossing my fingers behind my back, I knock on Lucky's door before cracking it open. Seeing the room is empty, I sigh in relief. At least it looks like he's letting himself be welcomed into the fold this time around. Pre-memory loss Lucky was paranoid and skittish and overly cautious about offending anyone. This Lucky seems to be more relieved at having his freedom than worrying about anything else.

Is it wrong that I don't want him to get his memory back?

When I turn to pull the door shut, the sunlight reflects off the surface of the watch he was so excited for earlier. Considering how important it is to him, I decide to move it away from the edge of the nightstand so it won't get damaged. Picking it up, I notice there's an inscription on the back I didn't see earlier:

To my Jo-meo,
You can ride more than horses with me.
Love,
Your Juliet

Uhhhh....

I hurriedly place the watch next to Lucky's alarm clock and exit the room. I just found out *way* more than I ever wanted to know about Joseph Grable, my good friend's father and my hopefully future boy's grandfather. How in the hell did Lucky's mother end up with such a stick up her ass if this was what her own mother was like?

My phone dings with a text.

> **Toby:**
> Hurry your booty up! We can't go to La Casita without you! Lucky insists.

I race into my room and change into my pajama pants and school hoodie. Time for some movie cuddles while the boys sing along. This is one of my favorite house traditions, and I'm glad to see we are reviving it. The last few months before I left for the program, I was too busy working. But that is done for now, and tonight I get to share this time with my boy. After all, he insists.

I race down the stairs, almost colliding with Eli coming in the front with about a dozen large pizzas. Judging by the smell, someone convinced him to grab more than just pepperoni this time. If I'm not around when they order, or Scott isn't cooking, most of these guys go for the simplest option available. We have an entire deep freezer in the basement full of things like dino nuggets and curly fries.

Grabbing half of the pizza boxes off his stack, I give my friend a look to let him know I want to have a talk later. He just laughs and strolls through the kitchen, heading straight for the basement stairs.

"Plates?" I ask while he balances the boxes to open the door to the basement.

"Already down there," he grunts after finally getting the door open wide enough for us to get through with the pizzas. "While I was giving Lucky a crash course on Kink Manor and its residents, Shiloh built a verifiable pillow oasis on the floor for tonight. I think he used every single spare pillow and blanket in the house.

"Jace and Toby carried down the food supplies while Scott set up the tables for our pizza party buffet after making his gourmet popcorn flavors…"

As we enter the theater room, I'm shocked at the transformation. Usually, we all pile onto the various pieces of camping furniture that we keep stored down here. If there's only a few of us, we will squeeze onto the old futon from my room at the Theta house, but it doesn't look like the same room. Shiloh made a nest of pure softness in the center of the floor. The subs all seem to be comfortable down there, while the singular futon has been dragged behind the nest for those of us not willing to sit on the floor.

Shiloh sees us first, and his look of worry turns into a vibrant smile when he realizes we like what he has done with the place. I hope someday he is able to find a man who will make him smile like that always. Our little kitten deserves it after what he's been through.

Toby is of course next to notice us, sniffing the air like the pup he is. Of course, the food catches his attention first, but then his gaze tracks to take in the people who brought it.

"Daddy Spencer is in da hiz-ouse! Time to start the movie!" As he starts to do a little dance, Lucky pushes him over into Jace's lap and scrambles to his feet to run over to me and Eli.

"Forget the movie," he says, licking his lips. "Pizza is here!"

32

LUCKY

Everyone got a good laugh over the fact that I managed to scarf down three large pizzas by myself. I want to tell them that three is nothing and that the only thing stopping me from eating more is that Jay hasn't had any yet. I even hid one of the pizzas just for him, since he was super nice to me at the hospital. So what if he doesn't eat all of it himself? Pizza will *never* go to waste around me.

When the credits roll after the movie is over, I'm feeling kind of sleepy again. I don't want to miss out on all of this fun, so I hide my face behind a pillow to let out a big yawn. I have the feeling if they notice I'm feeling tired, they'll put an end to the movie night, but I don't want my new friends to miss out.

Toby and Eric start arguing over what movie should be next, but when I look at Shiloh, he seems to be on the same page as me. He's curled up in a little ball on a pillow, looking ready for a nap. Maybe it's the kitten thing that means no one seems to care that he's sleepy...

Speaking of sleepy, Jay walks in with the worst case of bedhead I think I have ever seen occur in nature. He scratches his head and yawns out, "What's next? And did anyone save me some food?"

At the sight of the empty pizza boxes, he frowns. I can see him mentally counting the boxes when Toby runs over to him to tell him how I demolished three entire pizzas by myself. Everyone chuckles, even Jay, but I feel bad when he says he's going to go upstairs and make something before the next movie. I pull out the pizza I saved and jump up to stop him, but a pillow has schemed against me, sending me stumbling.

The pizza goes flying out of the box to splat on all of the people on the futon, including Miss Avery who turns out is the nice lady who did the news story to clear my name. She told me she even drove Spencer's car to the hospital when I was hurt the other night. But now she's got sauce on her shirt and mushrooms in her hair.

"I'm s-s-sorry," I whimper before running for the stairs. Jay is somehow quicker than me and gets his arm around my waist to scoop me up before I can even touch the first step. My tears are falling faster now, and I can't stop apologizing. Thanks to my clumsiness, their clothes are ruined. Jay doesn't get to eat. I made a mess that will take forever to clean up. Shiloh's pretty pillow nest is dirty...

I feel Jay push me into someone else's arms. Of course he's angry with me. I wasted his food. I try to push away so I can at least clean up the mess I made, but the arms around me don't let go. I need to clean it up. It's my fault. *I need to clean it...*

"Shhh, little one," Spencer mutters, rubbing my back. Oh, I guess that who is holding me now. "You tripped. It was an accident. And a hilarious one at that. I don't think I've ever seen Eli eat a green pepper in all the years I've known him and you somehow managed to get him to swallow one."

He pulls me back enough to look me in the face before asking, "Do I need to find a way to get you to eat your vegetables, too? Is it a family trait?"

I shake my head in response. I've never had an issue with eating veggies or fruit. Only thing I don't like is asparagus, but that is because it makes my pee smell funny. That thought makes me giggle-hiccup before it hits me.

I blame it on Mister Ash pulling cheese out of his shirt distracting me when it takes a bit to realize what else Spencer just said. "You knew?"

He shakes his head and answers, "I met your grand-father today while I was working on my case and put it together. I know Eli's real name."

I have the feeling I'm missing some details here, but Avery told me Spencer is a private investigator. It would be irresponsible of him to live with guys and not do background checks on them, right? Satisfied with my brain's limited critical thinking skills for the time being, I go back to worrying about the pizza when Jay speaks up.

"That's all well and good, but I'm going to go up and

make some grilled cheese," Jay says before turning to me. "You want one, Lucky?"

These guys will never stop surprising me. "But I ruined your dinner and now you have to cook. Let me at least do the cooking."

Spencer chuckles and rests his chin on top of my head. "Jay is worse than Eli when it comes to vegetables. You hid the only type of pizza he will ever refuse. If the green peppers and mushrooms weren't enough to deter him, the black olives would have sent him running."

I huff and stomp my foot when I look at Jay. That's not right. I don't really know why it upsets me that these grown men won't eat their vegetables, but it does.

"Daddies need to set a good example!" I say before stomping back into the room with the others. Plopping down onto a pillow, I cross my arms and mope. I know I'm throwing a bit of a tantrum, but it just isn't right that these guys do so many things just right and then do something dumb like avoid tasty veggies.

Toby crawls up next to me and rolls over so his head is in my lap with him looking up at my face. "We need a tie breaker. It's between these two," he says, holding up two different Blu-ray cases. Looking at both of them, I don't like either choice. I'm not in the mood for another animated movie, or one so recent... I scoot out from under him to crawl over to the bookshelves holding the movies. The bottom two shelves appear to be all movies from our childhoods or even before we were born.

I see a movie that I remember coming onto the tv when I was home sick once as a child. My nanny at the time, before Mother fired her, told me it was her favorite movie when she was my age. Some parts were really scary, but I like the unicorns and faeries. I pull it off the shelf and hold it up to Toby.

"Can we watch this one instead?"

"Tim Curry *and* Tom Cruise? Absolutely!" he exclaims, ripping the case from my hand to put it in the machine to play. When the opening song starts, Spencer sits down on the pillow next to me, placing another in his lap. At my look, he adjusts me so I'm laying down with my head on that pillow and a blanket over me.

"Sleep if you want to, little one," he whispers. "The movie will always be down here whenever you want to watch it."

33

SPENCER

Lucky has been at the house for a little over a week now, and I feel like I'm in purgatory. Every moment with him is pure bliss, but I still can't forget the look on his face the night he ran from me. It just doesn't feel right taking things farther than cuddling without him having his memories. The doctor says they could come back at any moment, or they could never come back at all.

"Will you just allow yourself to be happy and tell him how you feel already?"

Eli's voice startles me out of my thoughts, and I realize I've been staring at the toaster that has already finished with my bagel. As I grab my food and step away, Eli tosses in some frozen chocolate chip waffles and pushes down the lever.

"You just wanted the toaster," I say to him. "Besides, I want him to make an informed decision with all of the facts, not just what we've given him here."

"*Besides... meh meh meh, blah blah blah,*" he teases.

"Get your head out of your ass and talk to my nephew about this already. You both go back for classes today, and I need to know you have his back on campus... you know the bitch is going to find him there."

I growl into my coffee cup at the reminder that Sabrina Carlisle is still walking free at the moment. Since she is not a violent offender, the district attorney isn't in a rush to file charges to get her put in jail. He says he wants to make sure it's an airtight case.

I smell something fishy there, but the only thing I can do is keep an eye out while I dig deeper. I'm waiting for my cyber-sleuth buddy to get back to me on what he's found out. He will get me the breadcrumbs so that I can get the hard evidence. If only he wasn't on the other side of the country, I would be on his ass in person to get him to rush this.

"You all can relax," Toby breezes into the kitchen and goes straight for his Pop-Tarts. We've tried to switch him over to the store brands to save money, but he refuses. Considering it is one of only two of the name brand items he eats, I've learned to let it go. The other is Spagettios which I totally commiserate with him on that one. We tried the store brand once and threw out the entire can after one bite each.

He hits the cancel button on the toaster, pulling Eli's waffles out to put his toaster pastries in. I just raise my brows while our Sadist looks ready to kill. Toby, the ADHD puppy, just doesn't notice. Moments like this make me wonder if he really doesn't notice or if he is acting out because he needs some discipline or release.

He always seems better after a play session, so we might need to move up our planned house visit to the Devil's Club. We put it off after Lucky's accident, and then voted as a house to postpone until he is ready to go. We don't want to leave him alone until everything is settled.

"I managed to sign up for the same class as Lucky and have nothing else today until after Daddy Spence is done with his classes," he says as the toaster finishes his breakfast. "We got him covered for Mondays and Wednesdays. It's the Tuesday, Thursday classes that will be tricky."

Eli slides behind Toby to put his waffles back into the toaster and gives him a nice hard, well deserved, swat on the ass. The pup yelps in surprise which causes both Eli and I to laugh.

"Oooh, me too, Daddy," Eric croons to Eli as he walks past him to largest of the three coffee makers in the room. We are a house that loves our coffee, and in the mornings, not everyone knows how to wait for their turn.

"Not a Daddy," Eli mutters before grabbing his travel cup and naked waffles when they pop up. "Ash and Sam will be in the same building if not the same class for his Tuesday-Thursday class. I gotta go into the city today and see the lawyer. Dad wants to get Lucky's trust released to him early now that he is divorced and the bitch can't touch it."

"I thought he already had his trust fund and the puppy killer spent it all?" Toby asks, rubbing his left ass cheek. We all stop and stare at our own resident pup in confusion. At our look, he takes a big bite of his breakfast and explains while chewing. "Lucky told me when she first approached him she reminded him of Cruella, like the movie with the dalmatians..."

Eli just shakes his head and smiles before he snatches up a briefcase and heads to the front. While he's pulling on his shoes, he tells us, "Accurate depiction of Sabrina. But as for the money, Lucky had two trust funds. His parents, and therefore he, were only aware of the one *they* set up for him as a Holloway. Dad didn't want to risk Nadine getting her claws into this one before Lucky was old enough to fight her for it.

"It was set up to release when he turns twenty-five or graduates, whichever comes first, but Dad wants him to have some of it a little early to make this whole situation easier on him. As the trustee, I have to be the one to sign off on it. I'm not dissolving it, but I am giving him access to some of the funds as a monthly allowance kind of thing."

Toby is halfway up the steps before he turns to ask, "Why not dissolve it and give him all or the money?"

"Because we don't know how Sabrina is getting her information on me that she shouldn't be able to get her hands on," Lucky says as he passes Toby on the way down the stairs. "Putting all of the money in an account in my name means there's a chance she can access it through whatever she has been doing. Keeping it in a trust with me receiving an allowance means the most she's able to screw me out of is one month of whatever Eli sets up as the allowance amount."

Turning back around to look up the stairs at Toby, he further explains, "My grandfather has a net worth that could flat out buy my father's company ten times over and still not show a drop in his accounts once the next hour's interest accumulates on his investments. If my trust fund from him is anywhere near the amount he gave my mother, it means I have enough money coming to me to live extremely well for multiple lifetimes."

Lucky turns back to finish coming down the stairs and heads into the kitchen for his coffee. Eric has been uncharacteristically quiet over everything that has been revealed so far, but I hear him talking to Lucky in the kitchen. I have an idea of what might be bothering Eric, but that is his business to share or not with my boy. I turn back to Eli to wish him well, but he's smirking up the stairs.

"Looks like we might need a puppy reboot," he mutters before heading out the front door. Tobias is frozen on the stairs. If this was a cartoon, he'd have little stars flickering around him. I chuckle and leave him to his thoughts. I need more coffee, and there is a boy in the kitchen I need to have some quality time with before we get to campus.

34

LUCKY

My first day back on campus after a year away is surreal. Everything is familiar, yet not. I had barely gotten my feet under me finishing my freshman year, but now it feels like I'm starting over again. The car doors closing behind me snap me out of my thoughts, and Toby grabs my hand to start pulling me toward the student union. It is the *only* place on campus that can do the fancy coffees.

Rumor was that the guy running it used to be a student, but instead of opening a bakery and coffee shop in the city, he decided to continue with his work study job and just took over the place. I'm not sure how true that is, but the muffins are to die for...

And they sell out very quickly, which explains why Toby is pulling me with such force.

"Do I need to get your leash so you will walk correctly, pup?" Spencer calls out from behind us.

Toby stops and turns so suddenly that I stumble into him. We both go tumbling to the ground in a jumble of arms and legs. I somehow manage to shift myself so that I'm under the other man when we hit the concrete of the sidewalk. Better me get hurt than him. He's super nice and shouldn't be hurt because I ran into him.

"Oh my God, Lucky," Toby breathes out as he rushes to get off of me. "Are you alright? Did you hit your head again? I'm so sorry!"

I wave away his concern as I take inventory of my body. I can feel that my tailbone and elbow took the worst of the blow, but the slight headache makes me think I actually might have bumped my head. Before I can even voice my injuries, Spencer is pulling Toby away to take his place above me.

"Where are you hurt, little one?" he asks while running his hands all over me. When he gets to my arm, he pulls his gym towel out of his bag. "Close your eyes, Lucky. I'm going to get you fixed up."

I want to listen to him, but there is a morbid curiosity inside of me. I never used to be this inquisitive. I used to just do as I was told. Now, there is something that makes me want to know everything...

So, I look.

The fall ripped open the wound on my arm from the fall last week and blood is oozing out over the concrete.

I should have listened to Daddy...

The next thing I am aware of is waking up surrounded by the smell of coffee and chocolate cake. That can't be right.

"I think he's waking up." I can hear Toby nearby.

"Thanks for letting us back here, but we'll get out of your way soon. We have class in a little bit."

Groaning, I try to sit up only to feel a hand at my back supporting me and helping me turn to put my feet down. I open my eyes to see that I'm on a futon in some sort of a break room with Spencer sitting on the ground beside me. Toby is by the door talking to someone... oh, it's the manager of the coffee shop. I'm glad he's still here. He was always nice to me when I ordered my white chocolate mocha with cinnamon. He didn't think it was strange like some of his baristas did.

"How are you feeling, little one?" Spencer asks me, and I take stock of my injuries. Just like I thought from before, there's nothing too serious. I feel around the back of my head and there is a slight tender spot, but as long as I don't get woozy or dizzy, I should be fine.

"I'm good," I mutter. I almost call him Daddy, but since there is someone from outside the house present, I don't want to freak him out. "I should probably get to class, though. I don't want to be late on my first day back.

Spencer nods, not looking convinced in the least, but I appreciate him taking me at my word. I like the fact that he worries over me. The last week has shown me what it is like to have people genuinely care about me as a person. I've been included for once in my life, and I don't want to have to give that up.

"Time to go," Toby declares as he helps me up off the futon and drags me out a side door. Shoving a chocolate chip muffin into my hand, he leads us over to the economics building for our class.

Toby is a sophomore taking all of his core classes right away, saving his electives for his senior year. I did the opposite. Not knowing what I wanted as my major when I started, I took all of my electives freshman year. My parents want me to major in business, but I don't want to be a CEO or manager. I have a love of research and not dealing with people. Mother finally relented when father suggested accounting as my major, stating that Holloway Industries could put me in a CFO until he retires, and by then I will be established in the company enough to take over.

I hate the fact that they planned out my future without consulting me. It's like I am just a doll being moved around however they want me. I hate it. Spencer might make decisions for me as a Daddy, but at least he consults me and asks me things before making plans.

My thoughts are interrupted when I crash into Toby for the second time this morning. At least this time we were walking, so no falling involved. Looking around him, I notice that there is a new Economics professor this year, or at least new to me. Judging by my housemate's reaction, I'm guessing he's *new* new. I glance down at my schedule to check the name... Professor Lewis Barnes.

I shove Toby toward the risers so that we can take our seats. I put the muffin on the desk-top while I pull out my laptop in preparation for the class to start. Toby is still fully focused on the man in front of the room. Objectively, I can see that he's attractive, but I've never been a great judge of that. He's not Daddy, so that auto-matically puts him out of my mind. I elbow the pup next to me, and he shakes himself out before reaching into his own bag.

"Look who came back to school," a voice comes from the other side of the desk while I'm crouched under the desk, digging in my backpack for my stylus. I like to be able to draw diagrams directly into the computer if needed. "It's a shame you couldn't keep it in your pants. But then again, you rich boys never have to, right? Did you..."

I'm doing my best to ignore James, but a growl from next to me makes me sit up fast enough that I get a bit lightheaded. Toby is standing and glaring at my former roommate. The growl is actually coming from him. For some reason, I thought him being a pup meant some barking and playing fetch. I forgot that dogs growl when threatened or being protective... As touched as I am, I need to de-escalate the situation before Toby outs himself. James isn't worth the extra attention.

"Toby, it's fine," I tell him, placing my hand on his arm to pull him back into his chair. "He's just mad that Sabrina wasn't exclusive to him."

James explodes in front of me, throwing my laptop to the ground in anger. "What do you mean she wasn't exclusive? She never fucked you! You are a pathetic little pushover. She never had to even touch you to get you to marry her. She loves me and only me! You were just the money she needed to bail out her father's company."

The room goes silent except for my former roommate's panting. A few people have their phones out and I'm sure that before the hour is up, the video is going to be blasted all over social media. Spencer is going to have a field day with this!

My smile is apparently the wrong reaction for James. He reaches across the desk and grabs me out of my seat by my collar. He's gathered it so tightly that it is a bit of a struggle to breathe, and I'm clawing at his hands to try and get them to release. I hear yelling from next to me, but my attention is all on the enraged man in front of me and the fact that I can't get a decent breath...

The hands grasping me release suddenly and I would have fallen if not for Toby catching me. Looking up, I see Professor Barnes has James in an arm lock and is pushing him toward the door.

"Syllabus is on the desk and on the cloud," he says from the doorway, pushing James into the frame. "I'm taking this one straight to the dean's office. As for the rest of you, enjoy your free time. My class won't allow for much of it for you. Welcome back to Wrenshaw."

Toby and I are the only ones left in the room after about a minute. No one else stuck around once we were dismissed. I crouch down in front of where I was sitting and feel my emotions boil over at the sight in front of me. Falling back on my butt, I start to wipe at my eyes to try and stop the tears.

"Come on, don't cry," Toby hurries to pick up my things. "Eli said he's getting you some money today, right? We will go get you a new laptop tonight. Scott can help get you the best deal. When it comes to computers, no one knows more about them in the house."

The man in front of me is doing his best to cheer me up, but I just cry harder. I don't know how long I am inconsolable, but eventually my sobs turn to hiccups. At some point, Spencer must have shown up because I am in his arms. I like listening to his heartbeat. It's steady, just like he is.

"We'll get you a new computer, little one," he says, kissing the top of my head. I get the feeling he's said it a few times, but I push that thought away.

"I know. I'm not worried about the laptop," I manage to get out between the hiccups. "He smooshed my muffin!"

And for some reason, that sets me off again.

35

SPENCER

The first two weeks of classes are done, and outside of the first day with James, there have been no problems for Lucky on campus. Thanks to that incident, the entire school knows that Sabrina tricked Lucky, and he has gone from being the villain to the victim. For the sake of the courts, this is great. For my boy, not so much.

"I don't understand why people want to talk to me!" he yells from the passenger seat of my car as I turn onto the highway to take us home. "If all they want to say is that my ex-wife is a bitch, they don't need to. I am well aware of that fact."

I chuckle while he vents. Lucky is very much not a people person, so all of this attention is driving him crazy. I can't blame him. It was going to be bad enough after the newscasts, but James made it worse with his outburst. Now, Lucky can't go anywhere on campus without someone trying to commiserate with him.

When he takes a breath, I jump in before he gets

going again. "What do you say we all take tonight to go to the Devil?"

He sputters and coughs before responding with a confused grunt, and I chuckle.

"Remember the club Eli mentioned that we go to?" I ask. He nods in response, still giving me the side eye. "It's called the Devil's Club. It is a kink club that we all are members of. It's a perk of the house. The landlord has connections to it and hooks us up."

The boy looks nervous, but I can't help the smile that comes through on my face when he responds with a whispered, "I guess I can at least see what Eric keeps talking about."

We all get a release and a chance to fully relax going to the Devil, but some of us get more out of it than the others. Our resident queen needs someone to punish the brat inside of him. He needs someone to force everything out periodically so that he doesn't self-destruct his own life again. I don't ever want to see my oldest friend in that kind of pain again.

"Why don't you text Toby to meet us there after his last class?" I tell him. "We can run home and grab his pup gear and pick up Shiloh and anyone else at the house. If we need to, we can put a message in the group chat."

At my suggestions, Lucky perks up and gets to work on his phone. I can only guess what is going on in the group chat to have him giggling like he is, but after a minute, he looks worried. I put my right hand on his knee and give it a squeeze.

"What's up, little one? Where'd my favorite sunshine smile disappear to?"

He huffs out a frustrated noise before turning his head to me.

"I don't know what to do at a kink club," he says. "I know, or at least I'm pretty sure at this point, I am a little who likes cuddles and stuffies. But I can't reconcile that with the whips and chains and stuff that I have seen online for examples of kink clubs. I mean, I look at a Saint Andrews cross and the only thing I can think of is climbing it like a jungle gym."

36

LUCKY

Of course, I can't tell Spencer the real reason I'm worried about going to the Devil's Club today. I have been trying to build up the courage over the last two weeks to ask him to be my boyfriend and Daddy. I overheard him telling Uncle Eli at the end of that first movie night that he won't be with me while I still don't remember why I ran into the woods that day. Well, I remember now. And I feel really dumb knowing what I do now for having run away.

The bump on the head that I got when I crashed into Toby on the first day of classes must have knocked my memories loose because it all came back to me the following morning. The anger. The fear. The paranoia. The despair. The shame and embarrassment.

The last two weeks of my marriage were nothing more than a series of gaslighting and abuse to wear me down emotionally. When I was served the divorce papers at work, my father-in-law came to me less than a minute later to tell me I was fired. At the time, I thought he was angry with me, that I disappointed him yet again.

I went back to the house I shared with Sabrina only to find a notice on the door from the sheriff's office telling me I had twenty-four hours to vacate the premises. I rushed through packing only to find that my cars were all being towed away, including the one I just arrived in. I tried to call my lawyer, the one my father had work on the pre-nuptial agreement, but he was not answering my calls.

Turns out, my mother had informed him that he would lose Holloway Industries and all of the affiliated clients if he took my call. I only found that out when it was too late. Instead of someone who knew what they were doing, I was forced to get a fresh out of law school newbie thanks to my mother's reinforcement of Sabrina's smear campaign.

The hearing was two days later. It wasn't until Spencer told me that I found out that this was highly unusual and suspicious, especially considering I hadn't even signed the divorce papers when I received the notice for the hearing. Sabrina's cousin stayed at the house while I was there before the hearing to make sure I didn't take anything. I don't know where she was or what she thought I would take that mattered to her. But while Jasper slept, I started packing in secret and hiding the boxes in the gardener's shed. I couldn't risk him seeing me valuing something and having it disappear.

When we got in front of the judge, my lawyer just sat there, frozen. Sabrina's lawyer spun a crazy tale about me cheating and being manipulative and I couldn't say a word. It was my lawyer's job to defend me, but when the judge asked him about a rebuttal, he stuttered and sat down. I was shocked and upset at his incompetence, but he apologized profusely after the fact. I was his first case and he said he was pretty sure the other side missed some steps they are legally required to take, so he was completely thrown off. He said he was going to appeal, once he figured out how to do it.

The judge at least seemed pretty decent since he refused to give Sabrina everything. In fact, he opened up an investigation into how things got so messed up in his courtroom with my case. The accounts are still frozen until that is finished, but Sabrina somehow has total ownership of the house and cars.

When I got back from the court hearing, the police were at the house, denying me entry. I had to order another ride share to take me to the motel I had been visiting. Thankfully, Chris was a good guy and let me hide my cash in the safe there or else I would have had nothing. I still don't know how Sabrina continued to spend money over the last month or so since the accounts were frozen.

Even at the motel, I was constantly being harassed. Drug dealers and prostitutes kept knocking at my door, even after Chris switched my room twice. It was obvious they had someone watching me. After buying the car and paying for the two classes, I could no longer afford the motel room beyond a couple more nights at most, even with my new friend using his discount for me. So, I snuck back to the house in the middle of the day to grab a couple of boxes of my most important things from the shed and took off out of the city to find somewhere that the Carlisle family couldn't find me.

After the week I had, there was little left of me except for paranoia and fear. Everything was out to get me at that point because Sabrina had infiltrated everything in my life. There was not a single aspect that she didn't have a hand in. Everything was somehow only in her name, even though I remember the deeds and titles all had both of our names. She had controlling interest in every investment. Her father was my employer. Her friends were the only people I could associate with. I was her plaything, and she needed a new game to torment me with.

Between being overwhelmed and coming out of the panic attack, I was at my lowest point when I recognized Spencer that day. Thanks to the previous week, my first thought was that he knew Sabrina and was fucking with me for her sake, that he was going to turn me back over to her for her sadistic pleasure. The thought of her finding me, dragging me back into hell when I thought I had broken free...

I ran without thinking.

I was stuck so deep into flight mode that nothing anyone could say in that moment would matter. I was convinced that they were all fucking with me and were going to tell my ex-wife where I was. Reading the articles didn't help either. I had almost convinced myself that I overreacted when I made the connection that Spencer was her friend from elementary school that she mentioned in her interview. I made the decision that none of them could be trusted out of a survival instinct based on the psychological torture of the previous week.

Meeting everyone on a fresh slate without all of that extra crap weighing me down allowed me to make unclouded opinions on each of them, especially Spencer. Had I known then what I know now, I would have run *to* him, not away from him that day.

37

LUCKY

Turns out the Devil's club is that old supermarket just a quarter mile or so up the highway from McKinley's. I'm surprised when Jace, Shiloh, Scott, and Eli head into the woods while Jay and Eric join me and Spencer in the car. Eric tells me that there is a path through the woods that leads directly to the back door of the club and that when the weather is nice, most of them will hike down and back while one of them will drive with any gear needed for the night.

When I ask why the guys insist on going as a house instead of as individuals, Jay is the one who answers. "Some of us do go by ourselves," he says with a yawn. He got up earlier than usual to come out with us. "But we try to come out as a group primarily for the subs in the house. We can keep an eye out for each other better when there are more of us here."

Spencer adds, "Some of us get into more trouble than others."

"I resemble that remark," Eric pouts from the back-seat, causing Jay and Spencer to laugh.

I am feeling a lot better about going by the time we pull into the parking lot. After making the trip using the car, I can understand why the guys prefer to walk through the woods. For a club that is less than a half a mile away to drive home, we had to drive almost five miles out of the way to get turned around on the highway because of the concrete median on the road. By the time Spencer puts the car in park, the rest of the guys are coming out from behind the building.

Spencer and Jay grab the bags of gear from the trunk, and we all move as a unit to the front. When we walk through the front doors, I'm surprised to see what looks like a regular office lobby. There is a seating area, a couple of televisions mounted and playing what looks like music videos, and a person sitting behind a reception desk.

I am so confused.

A rather large man dressed in well-worn and practically painted on jeans and a tight black t-shirt comes from a hallway behind the desk and says, "Sorry to leave you alone, Clarence. Nature called and I couldn't hit the snooze anymore on that one."

Clarence, the person behind the desk, clears his throat and lifts his chin toward us. "Theodore, sweetie, look before you speak next time."

Theodore blushes slightly but doesn't apologize. Instead, he waves away the comment.

"It's just the guys from Kink Manor. We're good."

Eric glides forward and pats the larger man on the bicep. "Teddy, dear," he purrs. "We have a newcomer to the house. Mind your manners. He is family after all."

Clarence takes advantage of the bouncer's confusion and waves me over to him.

"Hello sweetheart," he says in a much gentler tone than he used with the other man. "My name is Clarence. You can use whatever pronouns you want for me. I answer to everything, including HBIC despite certain others trying to steal my crown." He smirks at Eric who returns the look with a rude hand gesture. The man in front of me just laughs it off, as does the rest of the room.

"If you give me your ID I can scan it and get the forms pre-filled for you. You're living up at the manor house?" I nod in response. "Good. I'll update that. Now, what do we call you? Not everyone goes by their legal names here and that is perfectly alright. And do you know where you want to go inside or do you need a tour?"

He hands me a tablet pre-loaded with forms for me to read over and sign. While I look them over, Spencer answers his questions.

"He goes by Lucky and I'll show him around. Don't worry about finding a replacement for the desk or a tour guide, C," he says. He shoos the others into the club proper telling them, "Lucky and I will wait for Toby. I got his gear with me here. We'll join you in a little bit."

Shiloh hesitates, but Scott and Jace manage to nudge him through the doors into the club.

Teddy, or Theodore, shakes his head. "Kitten still

needs his emotional support puppy, doesn't he?" he mutters.

"He's getting better," Spencer replies as I hand over the tablet with my signatures.

Clarence raises his eyebrows and shoots a glance between me and the man talking to the bouncer but doesn't say anything. I nod. Where it asked about area of interest, I filled out that I think I am a little. Where it asked about relationship status, I wrote in "Single but hoping that changes tonight." I haven't told anyone about my feelings for Spencer yet, but I couldn't help it. I need *someone* to know that it isn't just spur of the moment.

The man behind the desk gives me an encouraging smile right before the doors fly open to reveal our eager puppy.

"Sorry I'm late," he gasps out. "My driver refused to stop when he saw what the address was. He tried to lecture me on the dangers of places like this and I had to get out at the bar and walk it."

I can feel the anger rolling off all three men in front of me and it scares me a smidge. I wouldn't want to be that driver right about now...

Toby waves off their concern as he stands back up to his full height and laughs. "It's not that big of a deal. You know me. I always have energy to burn."

38

Part of me wants to run out and hunt down the asshole driver that abandoned our pup on the side of the road just because his destination was a kink club. But one look at Lucky's face makes me tone down my anger. Clarence follows my gaze and quells his own rage enough to where it is only visible to those who know what to look for with him.

Theo needs the slap Clarence lands on his chest for him to snap out of it. The big man looks more apologetic than he did when he was talking about using the restroom earlier.

"It doesn't matter if you have the energy," Clarence admonishes Toby, coming out from behind the desk to bop him on his nose. "It's not right to leave a cute pup like yourself on the side of the road. Nor is it right for a pup to be walking along the side of a busy highway for a quarter mile on a barely six foot wide shoulder."

I walk over next to them and grasp Toby's shoulder.

"There is a reason we walk through the woods and not along the road even though it might be faster. The highway isn't safe to walk, especially alone."

The pup hangs his head and whimpers out an apology. I can't take him being sad, so I thrust his bag of gear into his arms.

"Let's go to the changing room so we can introduce Lucky to the Devil's Club and all the fun inside, alright?"

The rest of us laugh as Toby immediately perks up and starts bouncing and skipping his way to the doors into the club. I just hope this isn't too much for my boy. Even if the club isn't for him, I hope this doesn't make him want to run away again.

After getting Toby decked out in his "public wear" gear, we head into the central area of the club. The owner set the place up with a lounge area toward the front of the building where if anyone somehow managed to get a look through the one way mirrored windows, they would only see some scantily clad people hanging out.

There is a bar, but due to the nature of the business, only non-alcoholic drinks are served here. If people want alcohol, they are directed up to Mac's up the road. The owners here have a great deal going with Eli for that one. Jace and the bartenders here, Ash and Sam, swap recipes for drinks all of the time. Plus, they will fill in at Mac's and vice versa when people need extra time off.

After about an hour of hanging out in the lounge, the guys start to split off to the various rooms. Shiloh and Toby head to the pet playroom. Toby will either find another pup to wrestle with or he'll run around the obstacle course until he's worn out. Shiloh usually curls up on a bean bag chair to watch. Usually, I go with them to make sure Shiloh isn't approached by anyone we don't know, but Eric follows them this time.

"Give the baby boy the grand tour, Daddy Spence," he waves me off. "One of you will relieve me in a little bit so I can have my own fun. Besides, with my nemesis out front, I have no one to show off in front of for a while."

Eli slips into the impact-play room while Jace heads to the bar to talk to Sam and the new guy. Scott looks torn between following Jace and going off on his own, so Jay puts him in a headlock to give him a noogie.

"Hey! What's that for?" Scott grumbles when he gets free.

Jay shrugs and asks, "You going to the playroom, or do you have a need to top tonight?"

Scott adjusts his glasses and harumphs before stomping off toward the playroom designed for the age players.

"Play it is," Jay chuckles as he casually strolls after our moody middle boy.

Turning back to Lucky, I notice his attention is fixed on someone across the room. Following his gaze, I notice Judge Roberts with a woman his age next to him on a sofa near the windows. Lucky doesn't look happy to see him here, and I don't want this to be what puts him off of discovering more about himself. I'm about to suggest we head to the playroom ourselves when the man spots us. He says something to the woman next to him before he gets up to head our way.

Lucky tenses beside me, but his face empties of all emotion. I haven't seen this look on his face before, and it almost scares me. Is this how he lived, hiding everything from everyone? My heart breaks a little more for what he suffered before finding us.

"Spencer Wright!" the judge greets me warmly before turning to the man next to me. "And this must be Lucky. Your grandfather speaks very highly of you, young man."

Lucky startles at the judge's words and I watch life start to bleed back into his eyes. "You know Gramps, too?" His voice is barely audible, but the pain in it is clear as day.

Judge Roberts hums an affirmation before continuing, "I've known Joe for going on forty years now. For the last twenty, you are all he wants to talk about. I was hoping to meet you much sooner than this, maybe bring our families together, but I seem to have missed that chance."

I choke on my drink. He what now?

"The only reason I wanted a closer inspection on that divorce of yours was the fact that I couldn't reconcile the man on paper with the man I'd been hearing about for the last twenty years. Now that Spencer here has finished his investigation, everything should be set to rights soon."

Lucky turns from the older gentleman to look up at me, clearly proud of me. I plan on getting that look from him as much as humanly possible from this point forward. The judge chuckles before saying his farewell and heading back to the woman I can only assume is his wife. When he sits, he whispers in her ear. She leans to look past him to wave at us, to which Lucky gives a shy wave in response.

"He seems much nicer than he did in the courtroom," he mumbles. "I was so scared."

39

LUCKY

It takes a few seconds for me to realize what I just said. When it registers to my brain, I slap my hands over my mouth. I'm so stupid! I had a plan where I would get Spencer alone and I would explain and ask him to be my Daddy. When he says yes, we would play... or get one of the private rooms Eli told me about and he can take my virginity. Since I know for certain now that Sabrina never touched me, I want Spencer to have that special part of me... even if I am asexual, I can still do it for someone I love, right?

Spencer looks taken aback by my actions. Did he not hear me? Is he going to take me home? I don't want to leave yet. I have plans...

"Relax, little one," he tells me, pulling my hands down and holding them in his own. "Let's go get a room where we can have some privacy and we can have a talk before our tour."

I nod and shuffle along behind him as he leads me off

into another hallway from the ones where the others disappeared. This one has rooms up and down each side. Painted on the door to each room is a picture or graphic depicting the theme of that room. We pass one having to do with doctors, a canopy bed, a bathtub, and a toilet before Spencer takes us into a room with a desk on the door. When he locks the door, I notice a light goes off out in the hallway.

"If the light above the door if off, it means the room is occupied. If it is on, it means free to enter," he explains while I'm still staring at the door from our side. "After an hour or so of the light being off, the front desk will call to the room for a safety check. They have a master key and can open all of the doors in case of an emergency."

"How do they know if it's been over an hour?" I ask. "Do they watch cameras or something?"

Spencer chuckles as he leads me to the loveseat in the room. I notice the room we are in is decorated to look like an office. The placard on the desk says CEO, but I've been in my father's office before. I can't think of a place less sexy than that.

"Can we get a different room? My father isn't sexy," I blurt out before he has a chance to answer my previous question. I mumble an apology when he huffs at me.

"Don't be sorry, Lucky-boy. I'm not mad," he tells me. "To answer your first question, Theo or one of the other bouncers does a sweep of the entire club once an hour, so if the light is off when they do their first sweep and it's still off on the next one, the room gets a call.

"Regarding the second question... We are in this

room for privacy to talk. Not that I don't find you ridiculously sexy, because I definitely do, but I don't want to put pressure on you."

"You aren't putting pressure on me," I tell him before he can speak again and I lose my nerve again. "I've been trying to figure out a way to ask you to be my Daddy for a while now, but I got scared. What if you really don't like me? What if you are only nice to me out of guilt? Or even worse, you're like this with all littles and I'm not special to you?"

I feel my panic rising as all the reasons why Spencer should turn me down start spewing from my mouth.

Arms wrap around me and tug me over into his lap. "Shh, little one," he murmurs while I try to get my breathing back under control. "It's alright. I'm here."

"There is a reason I won't be your Daddy yet, but it isn't any of those," he tells me, brushing his thumb across my cheeks to wipe away the tears. "Something happened the night you had your accident, and I can't in good conscience agree to be your Daddy when you don't trust me fully."

I sit up and shake my head so hard I almost fall off his lap. When he pulls me close again, I don't stop myself from telling him the truth this time.

"But I *do* trust you. I remember everything," I tell him and feel him still beneath me. I can't bring myself to look at his face while I spill the whole story. I start with the night of the Theta party and how safe he made me feel. I tell him about the fact that I had finally gotten up the nerve to talk to him but was ambushed by

Sabrina and my mother on the way to the Theta house that day.

I tell him about my father's total abandonment of me with the exception of making sure Sabrina couldn't kill me to get my money. I tell him about the rushed wedding and subsequent withdrawal from school at my mother's insistence. My time at Carlisle Construction and the regular gaslighting makes him tense even more, but that is only part of it.

I recount how Sabrina treated me every day and how I found out about her and James, with them laughing about me being clueless. I was never clueless regarding their affair. I only thought *better him than me*. I didn't want to have sex with my wife. I was already disgusted that I had already supposedly done it once.

My explanation about how the motel excursions came about finally thaws him a bit and he huffs a single laugh, but I'll take it. I was forced into a detour one day on the way home from work thanks to a water main break and saw the sign out front saying they offered the streaming channels for free. I was lured in by the cartoons, but ultimately ended up finding my freedom thanks to that random happenstance.

Spencer is still tense, but he still holds me while I tell him about the time I forgot, leading up to my fall in the woods. When I finish, I bury my face in his chest.

"I know I shouldn't have run," I mumble. "But I didn't have a chance to really think about it and I didn't know any of you. Then the article saying you were her friend... it was too much."

He plants a kiss on the top of my head and holds me tighter.

"I know, little one," he whispers. "No one blames you for running. Most of the guys in the house would have run in your situation as well. It's why we were all worried about you."

Pushing myself off his chest to lean back a bit, I look Spencer in the eyes and say, "Knowing what I know now, I needed that bump on the head and hard reset to see you and the others for who you really are. I would have never given you guys a real chance if I still had those memories clouding my perception of everything while I got to know everyone."

40

"I never would have been able to open my heart to you," Lucky says and pulls my face down for a gentle press of his lips to mine. "I really do like you and I want you to be my Daddy. Show me this new world and help me be the best little boy for you."

I crash my lips onto his in a fierce claim. His gasp of surprise is enough for me to thrust my tongue into his mouth. I want all of Lucky to be mine today, the man, the boy... it doesn't matter. Now that I know he isn't afraid of me and wants me, I will never let him go. I feel him go still in my arms and pull back to look at him.

He has a dazed look on his face, but there is a hint of something negative lurking. Did I hurt him?

"What's wrong, little one?" I need to know what I did wrong so that I don't do it again.

Lucky shakes himself like a dog coming out of water before smiling the thousand watt sunshine smile I love to see. "Nothing is wrong. I just spooked myself is all."

At my inquisitive look, he elaborates. "I've never had... um... *that*," he says indicating to the tent in his pants, "happen during a kiss before. Well actually, I've never had it happen outside of waking up a few times as a teenager."

"I'm not broken or anything," he hurries to continue. "I just never saw sex as something I really wanted to have before. But I want to know what it's like at least."

The surprise must show on my face because my boy's chin starts to wobble in the way it does before he starts crying. I don't mean to upset him, but the last thing I expected was to find out that Lucky is a virgin. Not only that, but I suspect based on what he just said that he might be somewhere on the asexual spectrum.

"Don't cry, little one," I mutter as I pull him in for a big squeeze. "If you really want to know what it's like to have sex, we can work up to it. But is that really what you want or are you saying that because you think *I* want sex?"

He sniffles and is quiet for long enough I start to wonder if he fell asleep on me.

"I want to know for sure," he says. "I've looked it all up and I am either asexual, which means I will get nothing out of sex but the physical release of the endorphins... or I am aceflux which means I might have times where I want and really enjoy sex, but I'm mostly indifferent to it."

Leaning back, he looks at me and asks, "If it turns out I'm asexual and don't like sex, can I still have you for my

Daddy? I swear I won't mind if you need to get sex from another guy. I just want to be your only little boy."

I gather Lucky in my arms as tightly as I can. How could anyone ever have mistreated a boy as precious as this one?

"Lucky-boy," I choke out, trying to hold back my emotions. "You are all I want. Sex or no sex. I want you to be my boy, my *only* boy."

Just when I think nothing will ever surpass this happiness I am feeling, I hear him whisper.

"Yes, Daddy."

41

SPENCER

It has been a little over a month since our first visit to the Devil, and Lucky has thoroughly blossomed as a little. In addition to cuddles and stuffies, we have discovered he also loves to color and play with toy farm animals. He is *not* a fan of cars or dolls. Video games confuse him, so unless he can button mash, he is content to sit on the sidelines to cheer on whoever is playing.

Finger paints and glitter are both too messy for him. He is a very neat and tidy little. His love of bubble baths can attest to that. Eli is talking about remodeling the bathroom in the basement so that it has a large jacuzzi tub so that Lucky can have his baths without forcing everyone else to use the tiny bathroom on our floor if they need a shower while he's playing.

I thought we might have a hit with playdough after he told me he used to love doing sculpting in art class in high school, but he can't get over the smell. Even though his wrinkled nose is adorable, I want him to be able to enjoy what he is doing. As a compromise, Eli and I surprised him by getting him signed up at the community college for a sculpting class, using some of his allowance. Turns out, his friend from the motel, Chris, is a student there and he's become a regular visitor at Kink Manor this past month.

Tonight, however, is the night of the Theta Halloween party, and as a senior, I am expected to attend as one of the hosts, even without living in the house anymore. Lucky is coming with me as my boyfriend, but he won't tell me what his costume is going to be. Because my boy is coming, that also means Eli is taking the night off to attend as well. Even without him being a student, I will do everything in my power to make sure he gets in. On the off chance something pulls me away, my boy won't be alone in that house ever again.

Pulling up the suspenders and sliding my arms into the navy trench coat, I have to give it to Scott. He always tells me I look like a taller version of his favorite television character, but I didn't believe him until now. I'll never be as fabulous as the character, but hopefully, I can pull off a believable pansexual immortal alien for the night.

"Helloooo, Daddy Jack," Lucky exclaims from behind me. "I'm kind of thinking I'm more on the flux side after all. *Yum-Me!*"

I pull him into my arms for a quick kiss before it registers to me what he's wearing. Taking a step back, I look him up and down with a smile on my face. He's wearing a onesie with a teddy bear and blocks printed on it and a pacifier clipped to it. He's got socks up to his knees and a pair of baby blue slip on shoes in his right hand. In his left is one of his new stuffies.

We had to set a limit on how much of his allowance from Eli can go to stuffies after the first wave of complaints from the delivery drivers having to come up the hill. Jay is getting him set up with a PO Box in the same post office he uses so that he can get his stuff delivered there.

"I'm so proud of you, little one," I tell him pulling him back against me. Running my hand down his back, I bite back the chuckle when I hear the crinkle of the diaper when I squeeze his bum. "Are you planning to use it or just wear it? I need to know if we need to pack a change or not."

He giggles and steps away to set down his shoes and grab a colorful backpack. It looks designed for a child, but it is most definitely oversized to make Lucky look smaller.

"Already packed, Daddy," he says, looking accomplished. "I also packed snackies and juice boxes and my sippy. Uncle Eli helped."

I mess up his hair in response but grab a pair of shorts for him before we go for the party. As much as I love that he is taking this step to try out diapers, I don't want to show him off too much. I can't help it if I'm a jealous Daddy.

We get to the house early to help with setting up since I am one of the seniors in charge. The house has improved greatly now that Adam and some of the other bad influences have gone off to the workforce. The remaining brothers were finally able to focus on their schoolwork instead of babysitting those idiots. I heard from Kyle, one of my pledge brothers, that the repair bill at the end of last year was only three hundred dollars and that was just a deductible to replace the carpet in one of the bedrooms. That is a huge step down from the almost twelve grand that Adam and his bros racked up the year before.

"Your boyfriend is adorable," Kyle says to me as we carry the last of the kegs into the backyard. "Is it real or just pretend for the night?"

I nearly drop the drum of beer I'm lugging when his words register. "What do you mean?" I ask cautiously.

Kyle smirks like I'm an idiot. "Dude, you are so a Daddy if I've ever met one. So, did you luck into Lucky the little or just Lucky?"

My answering smirk has him giving me a playful shove before we head back into the house. Once inside, I go in search of my boy when he isn't in the kitchen where I expected him to be. A commotion toward the front door of the house has my hair on end. Kyle takes off a second before I do when I hear it.

"Come on, little baby. I'll give you something to suck on."

I don't know that voice. No one should be here yet except Thetas and our immediate guests. And whoever the fuck is talking to my boy like that is going to get his ass kicked.

"Fuck you and the inbred horse you rode in on you insufferable limp dick shit stain!"

Kyle and I barrel into the living room just in time to see a guy about my size backhand my Lucky for talking back to him. Red coats my vision and I launch myself at the man.

42

LUCKY

Most of the guys at the Theta house laugh at my "costume" but don't make a fuss about it. A few give me looks like they *know* that it's not really playing dress up for me, but they don't say anything. Daddy's friend Kyle even gives me a wink to make me giggle. Overall, I'd say the first big public outing as Spencer Wright's boyfriend is going alright.

It would be perfect except there is one guy who keeps giving me the stink eye. Right after we got here, Daddy put me to the task of putting the child safety locks on the drawers and cabinets in the kitchen. Apparently one of the brothers in the past had a tendency to try and cook while drunk, so they started to do this for parties. As soon as I finished putting the last of the sharp and pointy objects in the locked cabinet under the island, Mr. Stink eye comes into the room with one of the few people I didn't ever want to deal with again.

"Well if it isn't the little bitch," Jasper Carlisle sneers

at me. "Finally wearing something befitting of a sniveling ingrate, I see."

I snort in response and move around the island to leave the room. I'll go wait in the car and tell Daddy we're leaving if this is the kind of crowd his fraternity will allow in.

"Big words from such a small brain," I mutter as I bend over to grab my backpack. I'm done being the punching bag for their family. "Your cousin should take some lessons from you. All she manages to screech out is *MINE MINE MINE.*"

I should have expected it. It's not like I didn't spend over a year dealing with his taunts and abuse. The hand in the middle of my back sends me crashing over a side table in the entryway. Standing up, I notice my binky came unclipped from my shirt. I look around the floor to see if I can find it. I mean I can always buy another one, but this one is the first one that Daddy bought me.

"Looking for this?" Jasper asks, twirling my binky around by the clip. "Come on, little baby. I'll give you something to suck on."

The rage that boils up inside of me is like nothing I've ever felt before. I used to cower before this man, and with good reason honestly. He's got easily over six inches on me in height and used to be on the football team in high school. But he's got nothing on Spencer. Where Jasper Carlisle is a has been, Daddy works out every day and goes to martial arts classes regularly.

Thoughts of my Daddy give me courage and I growl

out, "Fuck you and the inbred horse you rode in on you insufferable limp dick shit stain!"

Next thing I know, I'm being picked up off the floor by Kyle, and Daddy is in the front yard beating the ever loving shit out of Jasper Carlisle. Some of the brothers are trying to pull him off, but he shakes them off with ease. Seeing the crowd starting to appear for the party, I know I have to stop him.

"Daddy! I need help!" I call out to him, and he freezes mid swing. Eli jumps out of his car just then, and shit goes from bad to worse.

"Go help my nephew put some ice on his face," Eli growls when he approaches the men in the yard. "I'll finish this."

The brothers scramble back into the house, eager to get away from this new man on the scene, but Spencer just stares him down. Jasper is just a bloody lump whimpering beneath him. It's a battle of super testosterone, and I don't want anything to do with it. I turn around to get Kyle's assistance but see him frozen in place. The bigger man doesn't even flinch when I push him out of the way to grab my backpack. He is too busy staring at my uncle and boyfriend acting like it's high noon in the Wild Wild West.

I had intended to just wait in the car when Jasper Carlisle showed up and started tormenting me, but now I'm fucking leaving. I'm tired of letting everyone take away every single opportunity in my life. It was the Carlisle family for the last year and a half, but if I'm honest, I've been a doormat my entire life. It's time I fucking end this shit once and for all. Sabrina thinks I'm a pushover. She thinks that if she can throw enough money out there that people will cover up her misdeeds.

Fuck that. Mess with me? Fine. I could have walked away if it was just me.

This time, they fucked with the man I love. No one messes with my Daddy, even if he is being a dumbass right now and will need to do a lot of groveling when we get home…

The two men on the lawn don't even glance my way as I pull away from the house in Spencer's car. Plucking my phone out of the front pocket of my backpack, I make a call to set things in motion. I'm tired of waiting. I want my life back.

43

SPENCER

I haven't had a blackout episode since my parents' accident, but this time is so much worse compared to that. From what Kyle told me, I tackled and beat the bloody hell out of Jasper Carlisle on the front lawn. I have to believe it's true because videos were up on social media until about five minutes ago. Somehow every video of the incident has been erased, including the copy the police were supposedly sent to come investigate.

The police officer pulled me, Kyle, Eli, and a few of the brothers over to the edge of the driveway while the other brothers are inviting the guests into the house for the party. Jasper was already sent to the hospital with another officer by the time this one showed up.

"Until we get to the bottom of what happened here, none of you are free to go," the man in front of me says. "We were sent a video showing you assaulting Mr. Carlisle, as well as half a dozen calls about a man beating another brutally on the lawn here. So, what happened, Mr. Wright?"

Before I can open my mouth to answer, a luxury sedan pulls up to the end of the driveway next to us. The tuxedo wearing man who gets out of the backseat is none other than Joseph Grable, followed by an extremely pissed off Lucky. I'm sad to see he has changed out of his little outfit into a very expensive looking suit. He should have been able to enjoy the party going on in the house behind us. Instead, he witnessed the worst side of me come out. When I snapped out of my rage and saw my car was gone, I was afraid I'd lost him forever, but the look on his face tells me I'm not out of the doghouse.

"Officer Dowling, how is your mother doing?" Joe asks as he comes up to the man attempting to question me. The officer chuckles and gives the old man a hearty handshake. I feel even worse, having my boyfriend's grandfather coming in and playing the buddy card, exchanging favors, to get me out of this mess.

"She's doing well, Sir," the officer states. "She misses getting to go out for book club but the doctors don't want her driving until her hip is fully healed."

"Oh, if that's all, I'll send a car for her next week," Joe says before continuing, "And tell me, does she know that her son is taking bribes to harass upstanding members of the community while allowing abusers and rapists to go free?"

The man steps back in shock, color draining from his face. "Sir, what are you talking about?"

Joe waves Lucky forward, the swelling and bruising

already becoming apparent on his face. He's holding his side like it hurts him to move. Wait. When did he hurt his side?

"Is it not your name and signature on the report that my grandson filed against one Jasper Carlisle not two hours ago stating that the man pushed him into a table, threw him to the floor, verbally demanded fellatio, and then struck him in the face when he refused to comply? Is there another William Dowling at the precinct that I am unaware of?"

Joe is pissed, but he's playing the game. Eli, on the other hand, is being physically restrained by a few of my brothers. This is the first time he's hearing of what happened inside with Lucky today. Hell, beyond the crude remark and the backhand, *I* didn't even know the other stuff.

Another police car shows up and two more officers climb out. The female officer looks surprised to see the people gathered.

"Joe? Eli? What's going on? We were sent to find out what the hell Dowling is doing here instead of putting cuffs on Carlisle," she says. "The bastard slipped out of the E.R. before the officer following the ambulance got to him.

"Considering the reason Dowling was sent out here was the complaint filed by Mr. Holloway, there's no reason for him to be here instead of following up on the reason he was sent out."

Dowling flinches, but regains his composure before addressing her. "There were calls coming in and a video about an assault on the yard here at the same address. I show up to find the man who *supposedly* hit and said those alleged things beaten bloody on the lawn. I followed the clues."

Lucky steps up next to his grandfather to say, "You mean the clues like the fact that you texted my ex-wife the second that I stepped into the police station? Or do you mean the clues like the fact that you overruled the desk officer and took my statement in an interrogation room after turning off the recording equipment."

I can't lie. As pissed as I am hearing what Lucky went through at the police station, I'm really fucking turned on by this assertive side of him. I may be his Daddy, but my boy can take charge like this any day of the fucking week. Holy hell, I shouldn't be popping a boner in front of the cops.

"How about the fact that I was waiting on my grandfather to pick me up when I heard you on the phone telling the officer at the hospital to uncuff Jasper Carlisle before you even left to come to this house. The first officers on the scene did their job. They took statements, they recorded information. They stayed until they were dismissed *by you*, their supervisor.

"So tell me Officer Dowling," he asks with a cock of the hip that would do Eric proud, "How much is my ex-wife paying you to keep tabs on me?"

The officer in front of me wisely keeps his mouth shut and puts his hands behind his back. The female officer cuffs him and then removes his belt. As they load him into their car, I turn to my boy only to see a cold look on his face. Joe gives him a little push in my direction, and he sighs like coming to me is a chore. It breaks my heart and my dick goes back to its previous state.

"Talk to him, Lucky," Joe says. "I'll go speak to my son about his behavior. It won't be happening again."

Lucky steps forward to stand in front of me. He stays just out of reach and I am struggling to keep the pain from consuming me. I really fucked it all up this time, didn't I?

"Is there somewhere we can talk in private?"

44

LUCKY

Calling Gramps was the smartest thing I could have done in that situation. He walked me through exactly how to handle everything, from the police to the hospital and even the media. Avery sent me a text with the video of Spencer beating the shit out of Jasper and said it was sent to all of the media outlets with a simple story of him being my jealous and possessive lover taking revenge against my ex-wife's family because I was cutoff financially.

Thanks to Gramps's advice, not only is the video of no use, the media is now running the story of how my ex-wife's family is stalking me and bribing public officials to keep tabs on me, even after cutting me off and slandering me to anyone who will listen. The whole reason they refused to report on the things Spencer's investigation uncovered was fear of lawsuits from the Carlisle and Holloway families. Reminding them that I am the only grandson of the billionaire Joseph Grable seemed to change their tune.

In the car with Gramps, after getting picked up from the police station, I called Eric to see if he could get Spencer's car back to the house. One of the guys will drive Scott out to grab it later. Eric and Shiloh both agree with me that the Doms went overboard and fucked up when they ignored me.

While I was on the phone with the guys from home, Gramps called his friend Mike, who happens to be the judge who ruled on my divorce. He wanted to know why the hell the Carlisles are still harassing me. Turns out that Sabrina has been filing for continuations that the new judge kept granting. Well, Mike agreed it is beyond time to put a stop to that, so unless there is a *valid* reason for another continuation, the judge will make a final decision tomorrow. At that point, all of the accounts will be releasing regardless of the findings. The only thing his decision will determine is whether Sabrina goes to jail for grand larceny or if she just gets to go away.

Either way, there is now a restraining order against her, the entire Carlisle family, and my parents. I'm fucking done with all of them. The only loose end I have to tie up is with the man in front of me. He hurt me today worse than any of those fuckers ever did.

"Is there somewhere we can talk in private?" I ask him, hoping he will just take me home. There's no hiding from my disappointment when he heads inside the house and up the stairs. It only hits me when the door closes behind me that we couldn't go home unless someone else drives us. His car is still at the police station...

I recognize the room we enter. It's the same one he put me in when I passed out, but this time it is someone else's room. It's the same, but isn't.

"This is Kyle's room," he says in response to my unasked question. "He won't mind if we use it."

His voice is flat and emotionless, much like my own heart right now. There is too much swirling around inside of me to let the feelings take control. It would be so easy to just fall into my Daddy's arms and let him take care of me. But that would be a disservice to the both of us. He needs to know what he did wrong.

"Daddies make mistakes," I whisper into the silence to bolster my nerve.

Spencer spins around to look at me in confusion. "What do you mean, Lucky?" he asks with slightest waver to his voice. If I went by his voice alone, I wouldn't have the strength to say it. But there's terror in his eyes.

"You hurt me, Spencer," I tell him, plopping my bum... no my ass... onto the bed. I have to stay big for this conversation. "I called to you. I said I needed help."

Wrapping my arms carefully around my middle, mindful of the bruised ribs, I manage to choke it out. "You didn't listen. You ignored my call for help."

I watch as my strong and brave Daddy collapses to his knees like a puppet with its strings cut. He hangs his head in silence, but I can see the tears falling onto his pants.

I don't want him to cry!

Rushing to kneel in front of him, I grab his face and pull him up to look at me. I need my Daddy back.

"You hurt me," I tell him again, but there's more to it. I can feel the tears falling from my own eyes, now, but I have to get through this.

"You ignoring me hurt worse than anything physical Jasper has ever done to me. It hurt worse than all of the pain and suffering Sabrina or my mother or my family ever put me through. You. Shut. Me. Out. That is what hurt me, not this bruise on my face."

He pulls me into his arms in a crushing hug. I didn't have a chance to brace for it, so the yelp of pain I let out makes him drop me on my ass in a hurry.

"I probably should have kept the diaper on for some extra padding," I mutter, rubbing at the offending muscles. Looking up at Spencer, I tell him, "I ended up with a couple bruised ribs from the tumble over the table and just bruising and swelling on the face. Gramps already got me checked out at the hospital."

Gently, I climb back onto Spencer's lap and snuggle him while he releases the rest of the tears inside of him. Holding him close, I tell him, "Even Daddies make mistakes, but it just means they are human. You are still the only Daddy I ever want to have."

I stretch to peck him on the cheek before adding, "And make no mistake, you are *MY* Daddy. No one else's. Not now, not ever."

His watery chuckle is the best sound in the world to me right now. That means we are going to be okay.

EPILOGUE
SPENCER

"And do you swear to tell the truth, the whole truth, and nothing but the truth?" the bailiff asks me. I answer in the affirmative and take my seat on the witness stand.

The day has finally come, just in time for Christmas. Today is the last day of the criminal trial against Sabrina Carlisle. Her father took a plea deal in exchange for no prison time. Since the only thing they had him on was embezzlement of about ten grand and small time fraud that was mostly cleared up by his former son-in-law, he was small fries. He agreed to turn on his daughter, who had treated the company like a piggy bank. She was on the hook for over thirty million dollars, most of which was money direct from Lucky.

Over the course of my investigation, I discovered that not only did she conspire with James Buchanan to set up Lucky to force a marriage, she also had hired a hit man to kill her new husband after the wedding. We all have Mr. Holloway to thank for his foresight on that one. What was really surprising was what came to light earlier in the week.

Lucky wasn't the first guy she had pulled this scam with... He wasn't even the first one we know that she approached.

The prosecution had called Eric to the stand yesterday. I thought it was going to be a character witness testimony, but I was devastated for my best friend after they were done.

"Mr Mendleton, how do you know the accused?" the district attorney asks like he is discussing the weather.

"I met the bitch in elementary school when I called her out for extorting the other students," Eric says, looking extremely uncomfortable. "She ignored me until middle school when she started picking her dating prospects according to the number of zeros in their family bank accounts."

"Objection!" Comes the shout from the defense team. "Witness is proselytizing!"

The judge looks down his nose at the defense and says, "Overruled. The witness is sharing his own experiences and not trying to convert anyone to his way of thinking; however, the court will remind the witness to mind his language choices in his future responses."

"Sorry, your honor," Eric mumbles while the district attorney looks pleased. I hate seeing my friend up there miserable. I didn't even know he was supposed to be a part of this.

"Mr. Mendleton, have you had any contact with the

accused since you both became adults?" he asked.

Eric starts pulling at his fingernails which is a sure sign that he is getting overwhelmed and is likely to blow. I am trying to figure out a way to signal for a break before he does, but there's no one to notify.

"She approached me around midterms of my junior year, making a scene in the quad at my school," he says running his fingers through his hair. "She claimed I got her pregnant at some party, but that was impossible."

"Were you at the party?" the attorney asks.

Eric scoffs to hide the pain underneath before answering, "Yes. I was there."

"How do you know you did not impregnate the accused there?"

"Because I'm gayer than a rainbow in a designer shoe store during pride week, that's why!" Eric snaps before flinching and regaining his composure. "Sorry. That was rude. I am in no way attracted physically to the female form, so there is zero chance I would ever have sex with a woman, even one as butch as Sabrina Carlisle."

The judge bangs his gavel a few times to call the courtroom back to order after Eric's statement before telling him, "I won't warn you again, son. Watch the language."

Eric looks chagrined, but his leg is bouncing like crazy. He is going to do something very dumb if this doesn't end soon.

"Mr. Mendleton, is there any time at said party that you do not remember what happened?"

Eric glares at the district attorney before telling him, "I

remember every single millisecond of that party, and not once did I see a female in my vicinity."

He looks up to the judge with a vulnerability that he doesn't let show easily. "Can I please be done, your honor?"

My heart is breaking for him. The judge tells him he isn't done yet, but grants a recess so that he can get a break. I do the only thing I could do for my friend. I guard the bathroom door so no one else would hear his pain and anguish while he is forced to remember the worst night of his life, yet again.

"Mr. Wright, do I need to repeat the question?"

The voice of the district attorney brings me back to the present and the fact that I am on the stand now. I shake my head and answer who had hired me, what my findings were, et cetera. These were all things that should have been a part of my testimony in the divorce hearing.

"And when did you turn the report and photographs over to your client?"

I tell him and he does his spiel, entering the items into evidence which the judge and defense accept.

Then he starts questioning me about the deeper investigation I conducted into Sabrina and my findings of fraud, larceny, and a string of false identities that were used in previous marriage scams dating back to when she was barely sixteen. Three of those men died under suspicious circumstances, but the police could never find the wife after the initial interviews.

At the end of the day, it doesn't even take the jury an hour to come back with guilty verdicts on almost every charge brought against her. The woman is going to be behind bars for the rest of her days.

EPILOGUE
LUCKY

After Eric was forced to testify at the trial yesterday, I brought him home. He hasn't shared his secrets with me yet, and it is honestly his choice if he ever decides to do so. I just know that Daddy cried for our friend, and that he needed to be home, surrounded by the people who love him just the way he is. None of us have been willing to leave him alone since we got back.

I jump when the dinger goes off on the microwave to let me know the queso is heated up.

Eric already took the chips and our drinks down into the basement, so when I get down there he arranges our little fiesta for two. I don't really care what movie he puts on because this is all about making him feel better.

I don't even know why they made him testify. There was more than enough evidence against my ex-wife that it was cruel and unnecessary to make Eric take the stand. But the D.A.'s office said that his testimony shows that she targeted younger outcasts with money to run her scam. Her thing was apparently making sure the guy was at a party or gathering where there is enough room for her to cast suspicion that they could have had sex and him not remember it.

That didn't fit with the reasoning the district attorney gave for putting him up on the stand. He says he remembers that night. I have the feeling Eric wants nothing more than to be able to forget it based on the look in his eyes now. I miss Sassy...

I shake the bad thoughts away and squeeze my friend in a side hug, making sure not to spill the queso. Queso is sacred after all. Time to banish the shadows...

"Can we watch something with epic fantasy?" I ask him, giving my best impression of puppy dog eyes.

He gives me the first genuine smile I've seen in weeks and throws a chip at my head.

"Go pick one out, ya dork!"

He's going to be alright. Daddy and I will help make it all better.

Lucky and Spencer will continue to be a special part of Kink Manor. Eric's story continues in Drag Me Up, the next book in the Manor Drive Series.

ABOUT THE AUTHOR

I am a dog mom living it up in the insanity that is Northeast Ohio. When I'm not documenting the exploits of the characters in my head, I'm either binge reading the works of other amazing authors or losing my voice at hockey games. I'm horribly addicted to coffee, anime, and Asian dramas in addition to building my ever-growing stuffie army.

Kate Bauer is the contemporary alter ego of K.A. Bauer. I guess you could say Kate lives in this reality while K.A. is in a reality where mythical creatures and magic exist, and fate makes finding true love easier. All of her stories are LGBTQIA+ centric, and the characters fight for their rights and happily ever afters.

For the latest news on releases and appearances, check out my website www.authorkabauer.com and sign up for my newsletter.

I can be found on most social media sites under the username @authorkabauer

PREVIEW: DRAG ME UP
ERIC

"Have a good night, Sass!" Stacey's voice calls out from the hallway. Stacey is one of the dayshift bartenders, so she doesn't usually see the worst of what we can get at night. Plus, with her being assigned female at birth and identifying as cisgendered, she doesn't really understand what we go through to have someone recoil when they realize you have a cock between your legs. Nothing kills the mood like finding out your date is actually a dick-phobic bigot, probably so deep in the closet he's found a set of platforms with dead fish in the heel.

I wave absently in the direction of the door while I work on finishing the blending I need to do for my makeup. My look must be *perfection*. I will allow nothing less. The masculine falls away as the woman in the mirror emerges. Eric and all of his problems dissipate with each and every swipe of a brush or sponge across my face.

"Sassy, you're up next," Cleo says as she saunters into

the dressing area, breaking through my thoughts. "We've got you starting out with Britney tonight, since the elder millennial hooligans in the audience wouldn't appreciate the newer stuff. Betty and Cici are doing Gaga and Mariah. We're not touching any songs not old enough to drink tonight."

Cleo Lee DeStarr is my Drag Mother. She brought me in, gave me a job, and showed me how to be my most fabulous self. Outside of the club, he is Clarence Wilson, my frenemy to the extreme. Clarence kind of saved my life by introducing me to Cleo and the world of drag. But it still doesn't mean I have to like him...

Nodding to the queen in the mirror, I pull on my pigtail wig and stand to shimmy my way into the school girl outfit for the number. My makeup is already good enough to pull off two of the five Britney routines I can do, so I'll glam it up for the finale after the second number while the other girls are doing their routines.

Tying the knot in the shirt to reveal my navel, I feel the calm settle into me. Performing is the only way for me to relax these days. The last few months since the trial have been harder than usual, but being on the stage means I'm Sassy... and she doesn't have those memories.

Cleo blows me a kiss, and I flip her off before I flip my hair. I can't help but notice the concern in her eyes, and it pulls me out of the tentative headspace I managed. I force a smile on my face, hoping she doesn't recognize how fake it is. If she pulls me from the rotation tonight, I'm likely to go do something stupid to bury the memories again.

"Break a leg, Sugar," she whispers to me as I sashay out the door to head to the stage.

After my second individual number, I wave to Tyson behind the bar when I come off the stage. I need a fucking drink. Friday nights are generally good nights when it comes to the clientele in the Monarch Room Dance Revue and Gay Club, also known as the Mr. Drag Club. Tonight must be a full moon or something because the tips are flowing like a stream in the Sahara, and the audience is full of dickheads with their borderline bigoted catcalls.

Walking the floor is *not* going to be happening tonight. Most nights, I get a thrill and a much-needed dopamine rush from the cheering and adoration of the crowd. These guys, however, are more likely to send my mood six feet under like Lizzerati's unfortunate bedazzled recorder routine. Malcolm is a fantastic dancer and choreographer, but a musician he is definitely not.

Plopping my slightly padded ass into a folding chair backstage, I grab the battery operated fan off the shelf. I wish I could just go back to the dressing room to change and go trolling, but I still have to do the group number to close out the show. Usually, I would go do a wardrobe change and show off my most fantabulous self for the grand finale. This sea of cocknozzles does not deserve my best after how they've been treating each of us on stage.

"You sticking around to play afterwards or are you

going to head over to Pegasus?" Tyson asks as he sets my usual Sprite with a slice of lime on the shelf. "If you're sticking around, maybe we can..."

I wave hurriedly at him to stop the question before he can fully say it. I've been flirting pretty heavily with the new bartender since he started in October, but I never shit where I eat. He's proven that he is a great mixologist, and I can't fuck things up *again* for the club. The last bartender rage quit during a huge bachelorette shindig after he figured out that I am not the kind of person who will do relationships. I told him we weren't exclusive, but he somehow thought his cock was a magical cure-all for my issues or something. Cleo had to take the stage in order for Nick to tend the bar. The bride was *not* happy that Betty Whiteclaw didn't take the stage.

"I don't mess around with coworkers, Ty-baby," I croon to him, trailing my nails down his very muscular and tantalizing arm.

Don't fuck coworkers, Eric. You can't afford to lose this place, not now.

"As for where I'll be," I glance through the side of the curtain at the edge of the stage and spot Lucky, Spencer, Scott, and Toby cutting their way through the unruly crowd. "My guys just showed up, so I'll be around if you want to hang out a bit. But only as friends."

Tyson isn't fast enough to hide his disappointment before he nods and heads back out to his post behind the bar. Betty staggers off the stage while I'm still staring at the baby gay's ass moving through the crowd.

Part of me really wants to give him a ride he will never forget.

Don't fuck coworkers, Eric.

I know it's a bad idea, but a rather large portion of my brain doesn't give a flying fuck about consequences. Sometimes it really sucks being bipolar with ADHD. Being responsible is getting more and more difficult. I probably should get my meds adjusted again with the recent stress, but I keep forgetting to make the appointment. I'll do it tomorrow.

"...not even worth it to do the finale with this group. They're not gonna settle and they're making the stage downright dangerous with their spills. It's like they are on a mission to get us out of here."

Catching the last bit of Betty's whisper to Cleo, I am shocked. We *always* do the finale. Even if there are no paying customers, we will do the full show. I've never seen Cleo allow less, and I've been working here for almost four years. Hell, I've been coming here for longer, ever since my father ran me out of his house.

"I'm calling it," Cleo announces and pulls out her phone. After tapping a message, she grabs the wireless microphone from the shelf in front of me. Cleo becomes Clarence for a second, twisting her head from side to side. I hear the crack of her neck before she adjusts her posture from black-belt Clarence to her usually regal self and saunters onto the stage in the sudden silence when all the music is killed.

"Ladies, Gentlemen, and everyone in between," Cleo announces from center stage, her voice booming through the sound system. "Unfortunately, our finale performance for tonight will *not* be happening. It's time for our little butterflies to transform yet again, so please return next month for our new show here at the Monarch Room."

Next month?!

I can't take a month without performing! Not now. I need the distraction, especially with the trial bringing it all back to the surface a few months ago.

I race back to the dressing room and rip off my wig. I grab my phone out of my locker with one hand while I rush through tearing away the clothing, padding, and costume jewelry associated with Miss Sassy Frass. I'm leaving the makeup for now since it will work better to keep me anonymous when I pick up some nameless cock to ride for the night.

> **Kink Manor Queenie:**
> Going out. Don't wait up.

I hit send on the message to Spencer and turn my phone off before he can reply. Spencer might be my closest and oldest friend, but he would only try to tag along. I don't need the boy scout Daddy with his adorable ace little cock blocking me. I need to get railed hard tonight if I'm facing a month without performing.

"What are you doing, Eric?" Cleo's sugary voice calls out to me as I finish typing my code into the time clock to punch out. "It's only nine o'clock and you're on the schedule until eleven."

"Fuck off, Clarence," I grumble as I turn for the door.

He doesn't get to pull my safety net out from under me and then give me grief. I can find another fucking job if I have to. Hell, I don't even fucking need to work. Flipping him off over my shoulder, I head for my Mini-Cooper and race toward the South Side.

Fuck my meds. Fuck my job. Fuck all the people who claim to give a shit. I'm going to feel alive for a fucking change and to hell with anyone who gets in my way.

MORE BOOKS BY
KATE BAUER

MANOR DRIVE SERIES

A Little Discovery

Drag Me Up

Pet Project

Teddy Tea Time

Night Shift

No Pain, No Gain

UP/DOWN SERIES

Stood Up

Let Down

Trade Up

Down Play

Up For Promotion

WRENSHAW UNIVERSITY SERIES

Freshman Fifteen

Injured Reserve

Professor's Pet

Too Many Men

Dean's List

Frequent Flier

BOOKS BY
K.A. BAUER

ALPHA'S LITTLE PSYCHO SERIES

Alive

Holly Jolly Psycho (Novella)

Unburied

Afraid

Complete Series Omnibus

JAMESON PACK SERIES

Doctor Mate

Fated Mistake

Half Mate

Learned Fate

AFFILIATED STORIES NOT INCLUDED IN SERIES

Fated To Be Free